Selected Stories by
ROBERT LOUIS STEVENSON

Books in this Series:

Selected Stories by O. Henry
Selected Stories by Anton Chekhov
Selected Stories by Guy de Maupassant
Selected Stories by Mark Twain
Selected Stories by Edgar Allan Poe
Selected Stories by Rudyard Kipling
Selected Stories by Saki
Selected Stories by Oscar Wilde
Selected Stories by Honoré de Balzac
Selected Stories by Charles Dickens
Selected Stories by D.H. Lawrence
Selected Stories by H.G. Wells
Selected Stories by Jack London
Selected Stories by Joseph Conrad
Selected Stories by Leo Tolstoy
Selected Stories by Sir Arthur Conan Doyle
Selected Stories by James Joyce
Selected Stories by Virginia Woolf
Selected Stories by Thomas Hardy
Selected Stories by Fyodor Dostoyevsky
Selected Stories by Katherine Mansfield
Selected Stories by Wilkie Collins
Selected Stories by Howard Pyle

Selected Stories by
ROBERT LOUIS STEVENSON

Published by
Rupa Publications India Pvt. Ltd 2014
7/16, Ansari Road, Daryaganj
New Delhi 110002

Sales centres:
Allahabad Bengaluru Chennai
Hyderabad Jaipur Kathmandu
Kolkata Mumbai

Selection and Introduction copyright © Terry O'Brien 2014

All rights reserved.
No part of this publication may be reproduced, transmitted,
or stored in a retrieval system, in any form or by any means,
electronic, mechanical, photocopying, recording or otherwise,
without the prior permission of the publisher.

ISBN: 978-81-291-3527-8

Second impression 2019

10 9 8 7 6 5 4 3 2

The moral right of the author has been asserted.

Printed at Yash Printographics, Noida

This book is sold subject to the condition that it shall not,
by way of trade or otherwise, be lent, resold, hired out, or otherwise
circulated, without the publisher's prior consent, in any form of binding or
cover other than that in which it is published.

CONTENTS

Introduction	vii
1. Story of the Young Man with the Cream Tarts	1
2. Story of the Physician and the Saratoga Trunk	35
3. The Adventure of the Hansom Cab	64
4. Story of the Bandbox	87
5. Story of the Young Man in Holy Orders	114
6. Story of the House with the Green Blinds	132
7. The Adventure of Prince Florizel and a Detective	166

INTRODUCTION

Robert Louis Balfour Stevenson (13 November 1850–3 December 1894) was a Scottish novelist, poet, essayist, and travel writer. His most famous works are *Treasure Island*, *Kidnapped*, and *The Strange Case of Dr Jekyll and Mr Hyde*. A literary celebrity during his lifetime, Stevenson now ranks among the twenty-six most translated authors in the world. The short stories in this compilation have been taken from *New Arabian Nights*.

New Arabian Nights is a collection of short stories which include Robert Louis Stevenson's earliest fiction as well as those considered his best work in the genre. It is divided into two volumes, the first of which is composed of two story groups, or cycles: *The Suicide Club* and *The Rajah's Diamond*. The stories presented here belong to each of those cycles.

The Suicide Club is a collection of three nineteenth century detective fiction short stories by Robert Louis Stevenson that combine to form a single narrative. The trilogy introduces the characters of Prince Florizel of Bohemia and his sidekick Colonel Geraldine. In this cycle they infiltrate a secret society of people intent on losing their lives. *The Rajah's Diamond* is a cycle of four short stories by Robert Louis Stevenson.

- 'Story of the Young Man with the Cream Tarts' is the first story in the cycle *The Suicide Club*. It is set in the gas-lit streets of Victorian London where Prince Florizel of Bohemia and Colonel Geraldine roam in search of adventure.

- 'Story of the Physician and the Saratoga Trunk', the second story in the cycle, is set in the Latin Quarter of Paris where an American tourist finds himself embroiled in a dastardly plot. In the story, while lodging in Paris, naïve young Silas Q. Scuddamore is lured away by a beautiful young lady who promises a secret assignation but fails to appear. He returns to the hotel to receive a terrible shock.
- 'The Adventure of the Hansom Cab' is the third and final story in the cycle and is, once again, set in the gas-lit streets of Victorian era London where a retired British soldier looks for adventure. Former Lieutenant Brackenbury Rich is beckoned into the back of an elegantly appointed hansom cab by a mysterious cabman who whisks him off to a party.
- 'Story of the Bandbox', the first story in the second story cycle, *The Rajah's Diamond*, begins with the conceited wife of General Vandeleur sending her foppish secretary Harry on an errand. All hell breaks loose when Harry realizes the gravity of the errand, and the fact that what he is carrying are some of the most expensive jewels, including the famous Rajah's Diamond.
- 'Story of the Young Man in Holy Orders' continues from the previous tale, as although almost all the other jewels have been recovered, the famous Rajah's Diamond is still up for grabs. It is discovered lying on the ground by a priest, Mr Rolles, who is easily corrupted by it, and he gets into an uneasy alliance with a dictator, who is the brother of the owner of the diamonds.
- 'Story of the House with the Green Blinds' further unravels the plot in this story cycle, as it is discovered that the dictator drugs the priest in an attempt to wrest the diamond from him. However, his plans are foiled when the general's

illegitimate son, Francis Scrymgeour, appears on the scene.
- The final tale in this story cycle is 'The Adventure of Prince Florizel and a Detective'. This brings forward an interaction between the prince and a detective who has been sent to arrest him for possession of the Rajah's Diamond. The prince, however, devises a clever way out of the dilemma.

1

STORY OF THE YOUNG MAN WITH THE CREAM TARTS

During his residence in London, the accomplished Prince Florizel of Bohemia gained the affection of all classes by the seduction of his manner and by a well-considered generosity. He was a remarkable man even by what was known of him; and that was but a small part of what he actually did. Although of a placid temper in ordinary circumstances, and accustomed to take the world with as much philosophy as any ploughman, the Prince of Bohemia was not without a taste for ways of life more adventurous and eccentric than that to which he was destined by his birth. Now and then, when he fell into a low humour, when there was no laughable play to witness in any of the London theatres, and when the season of the year was unsuitable to those field sports in which he excelled all competitors, he would summon his confidant and Master of the Horse, Colonel Geraldine, and bid him prepare himself against an evening ramble. The Master of the Horse was a young officer of a brave and even temerarious disposition. He greeted the news with delight, and hastened to make ready. Long practice and a varied acquaintance of life had given him a singular facility in disguise; he could adapt not only his face and bearing, but his voice and almost his thoughts, to those of any rank, character, or nation; and in this way he diverted attention from the prince, and sometimes gained admission for the pair into strange societies. The civil authorities were never taken into the secret of these adventures; the imperturbable courage of the one and the ready invention and chivalrous devotion of the other had brought them through a score of dangerous passes; and they grew in confidence as time went on.

One evening in March they were driven by a sharp fall of sleet into an oyster bar in the immediate neighbourhood of Leicester Square. Colonel Geraldine was dressed and painted to represent a person connected with the press in reduced circumstances; while the prince had, as usual, travestied his appearance by the addition of false whiskers and a pair of large adhesive eyebrows. These lent him a shaggy and weather-beaten air, which, for one of his urbanity, formed the most impenetrable disguise. Thus equipped, the commander and his satellite sipped their brandy and soda in security.

The bar was full of guests, male and female; but though more than one of these offered to fall into talk with our adventurers, none of them promised to grow interesting upon a nearer acquaintance. There was nothing present but the lees of London and the commonplace of disrespectability; and the prince had already fallen to yawning, and was beginning to grow weary of the whole excursion, when the swing doors were pushed violently open, and a young man, followed by a couple of commissionaires, entered the bar. Each of the commissionaires carried a large dish of cream tarts under a cover, which they at once removed; and the young man made the round of the company, and pressed these confections upon every one's acceptance with an exaggerated courtesy. Sometimes his offer was laughingly accepted; sometimes it was firmly, or even harshly, rejected. In these latter cases the newcomer always ate the tart himself, with some more or less humorous commentary.

At last he accosted Prince Florizel.

'Sir,' said he, with a profound obeisance, proffering the tart at the same time between his thumb and forefinger, 'will you so far honour an entire stranger? I can answer for the quality of the pastry, having eaten two dozen and three of them myself since five o'clock.'

'I am in the habit,' replied the prince, 'of looking not so much to the nature of a gift as to the spirit in which it is offered.'

'The spirit, sir,' returned the young man, with another bow, 'is one of mockery.'

'Mockery?' repeated Florizel. 'And whom do you propose to mock?'

'I am not here to expound my philosophy,' replied the other, 'but to distribute these cream tarts. If I mention that I heartily include myself in the ridicule of the transaction, I hope you will consider honour satisfied and condescend. If not, you will constrain me to eat my twenty-eighth, and I own to being weary of the exercise.'

'You touch me,' said the prince, 'and I have all the will in the world to rescue you from this dilemma, but upon one condition. If my friend and I eat your cakes—for which we have neither of us any natural inclination—we shall expect you to join us at supper by way of recompense.'

The young man seemed to reflect.

'I have still several dozen upon hand,' he said at last; 'and that will make it necessary for me to visit several more bars before my great affair is concluded. This will take some time; and if you are hungry—'

The prince interrupted him with a polite gesture.

'My friend and I will accompany you,' he said; 'for we have already a deep interest in your very agreeable mode of passing an evening. And now that the preliminaries of peace are settled, allow me to sign the treaty for both.'

And the prince swallowed the tart with the best grace imaginable.

'It is delicious,' said he.

'I perceive you are a connoisseur,' replied the young man.

Colonel Geraldine likewise did honour to the pastry; and every one in that bar having now either accepted or refused his delicacies, the young man with the cream tarts led the way to another and similar establishment. The two commissionaires, who seemed to have grown accustomed to their absurd employment, followed immediately after; and the prince and the colonel brought up the rear, arm in arm, and smiling to each other as they went. In this order the company visited two other taverns, where scenes were enacted of a like nature to that already described—some refusing, some accepting, the favours of this vagabond hospitality, and the young man himself eating each rejected tart.

On leaving the third saloon the young man counted his store. There were but nine remaining, three in one tray and six in the other.

'Gentlemen,' said he, addressing himself to his two new followers, 'I am unwilling to delay your supper. I am positively sure you must be hungry. I feel that I owe you a special consideration. And on this great day for me, when I am closing a career of folly by my most conspicuously silly action, I wish to behave handsomely to all who give me countenance. Gentlemen, you shall wait no longer. Although my constitution is shattered by previous excesses, at the risk of my life I liquidate the suspensory condition.'

With these words he crushed the nine remaining tarts into his mouth, and swallowed them at a single movement each. Then, turning to the commissionaires, he gave them a couple of sovereigns.

'I have to thank you,' said he, 'for your extraordinary patience.'

And he dismissed them with a bow apiece. For some seconds he stood looking at the purse from which he had just paid his assistants, then, with a laugh, he tossed it into the middle of the street, and signified his readiness for supper.

In a small French restaurant in Soho, which had enjoyed an exaggerated reputation for some little while, but had already begun to be forgotten, and in a private room up two pairs of stairs, the three companions made a very elegant supper, and drank three or four bottles of champagne, talking the while upon indifferent subjects. The young man was fluent and gay, but he laughed louder than was natural in a person of polite breeding; his hands trembled violently, and his voice took sudden and surprising inflections, which seemed to be independent of his will. The dessert had been cleared away, and all three had lighted their cigars, when the prince addressed him in these words:

'You will, I am sure, pardon my curiosity. What I have seen of you has greatly pleased but even more puzzled me. And though I should be loth to seem indiscreet, I must tell you that my friend and I are persons very well worthy to be entrusted with a secret. We have many of our own, which we are continually revealing to improper ears. And if, as I suppose, your story is a silly one, you need have no delicacy with us, who are two of the silliest men in England. My name is Godall, Theophilus Godall; my friend is Major Alfred Hammersmith—or at least, such is the name by which he chooses to be known. We pass our lives entirely in the search for extravagant adventures; and there is no extravagance with which we are not capable of sympathy.'

'I like you, Mr Godall,' returned the young man; 'you

inspire me with a natural confidence; and I have not the slightest objection to your friend the major, whom I take to be a nobleman in masquerade. At least, I am sure he is no soldier.'

The Colonel smiled at this compliment to the perfection of his art; and the young man went on in a more animated manner.

'There is every reason why I should not tell you my story. Perhaps that is just the reason why I am going to do so. At least, you seem so well prepared to hear a tale of silliness that I cannot find it in my heart to disappoint you. My name, in spite of your example, I shall keep to myself. My age is not essential to the narrative. I am descended from my ancestors by ordinary generation, and from them I inherited the very eligible human tenement which I still occupy and a fortune of three hundred pounds a year. I suppose they also handed on to me a hare-brain humour, which it has been my chief delight to indulge. I received a good education. I can play the violin nearly well enough to earn money in the orchestra of a penny gaff, but not quite. The same remark applies to the flute and the French horn. I learned enough of whist to lose about a hundred a year at that scientific game. My acquaintance with French was sufficient to enable me to squander money in Paris with almost the same facility as in London. In short, I am a person full of manly accomplishments. I have had every sort of adventure, including a duel about nothing. Only two months ago, I met a young lady exactly suited to my taste in mind and body; I found my heart melt; I saw that I had come upon my fate at last, and was in the way to fall in love. But when I came to reckon up what remained to me of my capital, I found it amounted to something less than four hundred pounds! I ask you fairly— can a man who respects himself fall in love on four hundred pounds? I concluded, certainly not; left the presence of my charmer, and slightly accelerating my usual rate of expenditure, came this morning to my last eighty pounds. This I divided into two equal parts; forty I reserved for a particular purpose; the remaining forty I was to dissipate before the night. I have passed a very entertaining day, and played many farces besides that of the cream tarts which procured me the advantage of your acquaintance; for I was determined, as I told you, to bring a foolish career to a still more foolish conclusion; and when you saw me throw my purse into the street, the forty pounds were at an end. Now you know me as well as I know myself: a fool, but consistent in his folly; and, as I will ask you to believe, neither a whimperer nor a coward.'

From the whole tone of the young man's statement it was plain that he harboured very bitter and contemptuous thoughts about himself. His auditors were led to imagine that his love affair was nearer his heart than he admitted, and that he had a design on his own life. The farce of the cream tarts began to have very much the air of a tragedy in disguise.

'Why, is this not odd,' broke out Geraldine, giving a look to Prince Florizel, 'that we three fellows should have met by the merest accident in so large a wilderness as London, and should be so nearly in the same condition?'

'How?' cried the young man. 'Are you, too, ruined? Is this supper a folly like my cream tarts? Has the devil brought three of his own together for a last carouse?'

'The devil, depend upon it, can sometimes do a very gentlemanly thing,' returned Prince Florizel; 'and I am so much touched by this coincidence, that, although we are not entirely in the same case, I am going to put an end to the disparity. Let your heroic treatment of the last cream tarts be my example.'

So saying, the Prince drew out his purse and took from it a small bundle of banknotes.

'You see, I was a week or so behind you, but I mean to catch you up and come neck and neck into the winning post,' he continued. 'This,' laying one of the notes upon the table, 'will suffice for the bill. As for the rest—'

He tossed them into the fire, and they went up the chimney in a single blaze.

The young man tried to catch his arm, but as the table was between them his interference came too late.

'Unhappy man,' he cried, 'you should not have burned them all! You should have kept forty pounds.'

'Forty pounds!' repeated the prince. 'Why, in heaven's name, forty pounds?'

'Why not eighty?' cried the colonel; 'for to my certain knowledge there must have been a hundred in the bundle.'

'It was only forty pounds he needed,' said the young man gloomily. 'But without them there is no admission. The rule is strict. Forty pounds for each. Accursed life, where a man cannot even die without money!'

The prince and the colonel exchanged glances. 'Explain yourself,' said the latter. 'I have still a pocketbook tolerably well lined, and I need not say how readily I should share my wealth with Godall. But I must know to what end: you must certainly tell us what you mean.'

The young man seemed to awaken; he looked uneasily from one to the other, and his face flushed deeply.

'You are not fooling me?' he asked. 'You are indeed ruined men like me?'

'Indeed, I am for my part,' replied the colonel.

'And for mine,' said the prince, 'I have given you proof. Who but a ruined man would throw his notes into the fire? The action speaks for itself.'

'A ruined man—yes,' returned the other suspiciously, 'or else a millionaire.'

'Enough, sir,' said the prince; 'I have said so, and I am not accustomed to have my word remain in doubt.'

'Ruined?' said the young man. 'Are you ruined, like me? Are you, after a life of indulgence, come to such a pass that you can only indulge yourself in one thing more? Are you'—he kept lowering his voice as he went on—'are you going to give yourselves that last indulgence? Are you going to avoid the consequences of your folly by the one infallible and easy path? Are you going to give the slip to the sheriff's officers of conscience by the one open door?'

Suddenly he broke off and attempted to laugh.

'Here is your health!' he cried, emptying his glass, 'and good night to you, my merry ruined men.'

Colonel Geraldine caught him by the arm as he was about to rise.

'You lack confidence in us,' he said, 'and you are wrong. To all your questions I make answer in the affirmative. But I am not so timid, and can speak the Queen's English plainly. We too, like yourself, have had enough of life, and are determined to die. Sooner or later, alone or together, we meant to seek out death and beard him where he lies ready. Since we have met you, and your case is more pressing, let it be tonight—and at once—and, if you will, all three together. Such a penniless trio,' he cried, 'should go arm in arm into the halls of Pluto, and give each other some countenance among the shades!'

Geraldine had hit exactly on the manners and intonations that became the part he was playing. The prince himself was disturbed, and looked over at his confidant with a shade of doubt. As for the young man, the flush came back darkly into his cheek, and his eyes threw out a spark of light.

'You are the men for me!' he cried, with an almost terrible gaiety. 'Shake hands upon the bargain!' (his hand was cold and wet). 'You little know in what a company you will begin the march! You little know in what a happy moment for yourselves you partook of my cream tarts! I am only a unit, but I am a unit in an army. I know Death's private door. I am one of his familiars, and can show you into eternity without ceremony and yet without scandal.'

They called upon him eagerly to explain his meaning.

'Can you muster eighty pounds between you?' he demanded.

Geraldine ostentatiously consulted his pocketbook, and replied in the affirmative.

'Fortunate beings!' cried the young man. 'Forty pounds is the entry money of the Suicide Club.'

'The Suicide Club,' said the prince, 'why, what the devil is that?'

'Listen,' said the young man; 'this is the age of conveniences, and I have to tell you of the last perfection of the sort. We have affairs in different places; and hence railways were invented. Railways separated us infallibly from our friends; and so telegraphs were made that we might communicate speedier at great distances. Even in hotels we have lifts to spare us a climb of some hundred steps. Now, we know that life is only a stage to play the fool upon as long as the part amuses us. There was one more convenience lacking to modern comfort; a decent, easy way to quit that stage; the back stairs to liberty; or, as I said this moment, Death's private door. This, my two fellow rebels, is supplied by the Suicide Club. Do not suppose that you and I are alone, or even exceptional in the highly reasonable desire that we profess. A large number of our fellowmen, who have grown heartily sick of the performance in which they are expected to join daily and all their lives long, are only kept from flight by one or two considerations. Some have families who would be shocked, or even blamed, if the matter became public; others have a weakness at heart and recoil from the circumstances of death. That is, to some extent, my own experience. I cannot put a pistol to my head and draw the trigger; for something stronger than myself withholds the act; and although I loathe life, I have not strength enough in my body to take hold of death and be done with it. For such as I, and for all who desire to be out of the coil without posthumous scandal, the Suicide Club has been inaugurated. How this has been managed, what is its history, or what may be its ramifications in other lands, I am myself uninformed; and what I know of its constitution, I am not at liberty to communicate to you. To this extent, however, I am at your service. If you are truly tired of life, I will introduce you tonight to a meeting; and if not tonight, at least some time within the week, you will be easily relieved of your existences. It is now (consulting his watch) eleven; by half past, at latest, we must leave this place; so that you have half an hour before you to consider my proposal. It is more serious than a cream tart,' he added, with a smile; 'and I suspect more palatable.'

'More serious, certainly,' returned Colonel Geraldine; 'and as it is so much more so, will you allow me five minutes' speech in private with my friend, Mr Godall?'

'It is only fair,' answered the young man. 'If you will permit, I will retire.'

'You will be very obliging,' said the colonel.

As soon as the two were alone—'What,' said Prince Florizel, 'is the use of this confabulation, Geraldine? I see you are flurried, whereas my mind is very tranquilly made up. I will see the end of this.'

'Your Highness,' said the colonel, turning pale; 'let me ask you to consider the importance of your life, not only to your friends, but to the public interest. "If not tonight," said this madman; but supposing that tonight some irreparable disaster were to overtake your Highness's person, what, let me ask you, what would be my despair, and what the concern and disaster of a great nation?'

'I will see the end of this,' repeated the prince in his most deliberate tones; 'and have the kindness, Colonel Geraldine, to remember and respect your word of honour as a gentleman. Under no circumstances, recollect, nor without my special authority, are you to betray the incognito under which I choose to go abroad. These were my commands, which I now reiterate. And now,' he added, 'let me ask you to call for the bill.'

Colonel Geraldine bowed in submission; but he had a very white face as he summoned the young man of the cream tarts, and issued his directions to the waiter. The prince preserved his undisturbed demeanour, and described a Palais Royal farce to the young suicide with great humour and gusto. He avoided the colonel's appealing looks without ostentation, and selected another cheroot with more than usual care. Indeed, he was now the only man of the party who kept any command over his nerves.

The bill was discharged, the prince giving the whole change of the note to the astonished waiter; and the three drove off in a four-wheeler. They were not long upon the way before the cab stopped at the entrance to a rather dark court. Here all descended.

After Geraldine had paid the fare, the young man turned, and addressed Prince Florizel as follows:

'It is still time, Mr Godall, to make good your escape into thraldom. And for you too, Major Hammersmith. Reflect well before you take another step; and if your hearts say no—here are the crossroads.'

'Lead on, sir,' said the prince. 'I am not the man to go back from a thing once said.'

'Your coolness does me good,' replied their guide. 'I have never seen any one so unmoved at this conjuncture; and yet you are not the first whom I have escorted to this door. More than one of my friends has preceded me, where I knew I must shortly follow. But this is of no interest to you. Wait me here for only a few moments; I shall return as soon as I have arranged the preliminaries of your introduction.'

And with that the young man, waving his hand to his companions, turned into the court, entered a doorway and disappeared.

'Of all our follies,' said Colonel Geraldine in a low voice, 'this is the wildest and most dangerous.'

'I perfectly believe so,' returned the prince.

'We have still,' pursued the colonel, 'a moment to ourselves. Let me beseech your Highness to profit by the opportunity and retire. The consequences of this step are so dark, and may be so grave, that I feel myself justified in pushing a little farther than usual the liberty which your Highness is so condescending as to allow me in private.'

'Am I to understand that Colonel Geraldine is afraid?' asked his Highness, taking his cheroot from his lips, and looking keenly into the other's face.

'My fear is certainly not personal,' replied the other proudly; 'of that your Highness may rest well assured.'

'I had supposed as much,' returned the prince, with undisturbed good humour; 'but I was unwilling to remind you of the difference in our stations. No more—no more,' he added, seeing Geraldine about to apologize, 'you stand excused.'

And he smoked placidly, leaning against a railing, until the young man returned.

'Well,' he asked, 'has our reception been arranged?'

'Follow me,' was the reply. 'The president will see you in the cabinet. And let me warn you to be frank in your answers. I have stood your guarantee; but the club requires a searching inquiry before admission; for, the indiscretion of a single member would lead to the dispersion of the whole society for ever.'

The prince and Geraldine put their heads together for a

moment. 'Bear me out in this,' said the one; and 'bear me out in that,' said the other; and by boldly taking up the characters of men with whom both were acquainted, they had come to an agreement in a twinkling, and were ready to follow their guide into the president's cabinet.

There were no formidable obstacles to pass. The outer door stood open; the door of the cabinet was ajar; and there, in a small but very high apartment, the young man left them once more.

'He will be here immediately,' he said, with a nod, as he disappeared.

Voices were audible in the cabinet through the folding doors which formed one end; and now and then the noise of a champagne cork, followed by a burst of laughter, intervened among the sounds of conversation. A single tall window looked out upon the river and the embankment; and by the disposition of the lights, they judged themselves not far from Charing Cross station. The furniture was scanty, and the coverings worn to the thread; and there was nothing movable except a handbell in the centre of a round table, and the hats and coats of a considerable party hung round the wall on pegs.

'What sort of a den is this?' said Geraldine.

'That is what I have come to see,' replied the prince. 'If they keep live devils on the premises, the thing may grow amusing.'

Just then the folding door was opened no more than was necessary for the passage of a human body; and there entered at the same moment a louder buzz of talk, and the redoubtable president of the Suicide Club. The president was a man of fifty or upwards; large and rambling in his gait, with shaggy side whiskers, a bald top to his head, and a veiled grey eye, which now and then emitted a twinkle. His mouth, which embraced a large cigar, he kept continually screwing round and round and from side to side, as he looked sagaciously and coldly at the strangers. He was dressed in light tweeds, with his neck very open in a striped shirt collar; and carried a minute book under one arm.

'Good evening,' said he, after he had closed the door behind him. 'I am told you wish to speak with me.'

'We have a desire, sir, to join the Suicide Club,' replied the colonel.

The president rolled his cigar about in his mouth. 'What is that?' he said abruptly.

'Pardon me,' returned the colonel, 'but I believe you are the person best qualified to give us information on that point.'

'I?' cried the president. 'A Suicide Club? Come, come! This is a frolic for All Fools' Day. I can make allowances for gentlemen who get merry in their liquor; but let there be an end to this.'

'Call your club what you will,' said the colonel, 'you have some company behind these doors, and we insist on joining it.'

'Sir,' returned the president curtly, 'you have made a mistake. This is a private house, and you must leave it instantly.'

The prince had remained quietly in his seat throughout this little colloquy; but now, when the colonel looked over to him, as much as to say, 'Take your answer and come away, for God's sake!' he drew his cheroot from his mouth, and spoke:

'I have come here,' said he, 'upon the invitation of a friend of yours. He has doubtless informed you of my intention in thus intruding on your party. Let me remind you that a person in my circumstances has exceedingly little to bind him, and is not at all likely to tolerate much rudeness. I am a very quiet man, as a usual thing; but, my dear sir, you are either going to oblige me in the little matter of which you are aware, or you shall very bitterly repent that you ever admitted me to your antechamber.'

The president laughed aloud.

'That is the way to speak,' said he. 'You are a man who is

a man. You know the way to my heart, and can do what you like with me. Will you,' he continued, addressing Geraldine, 'will you step aside for a few minutes? I shall finish first with your companion, and some of the club's formalities require to be fulfilled in private.'

With these words he opened the door of a small closet, into which he shut the colonel.

'I believe in you,' he said to Florizel, as soon as they were alone; 'but are you sure of your friend?'

'Not so sure as I am of myself, though he has more cogent reasons,' answered Florizel, 'but sure enough to bring him here without alarm. He has had enough to cure the most tenacious man of life. He was cashiered the other day for cheating at cards.'

'A good reason, I daresay,' replied the president; 'at least, we have another in the same case, and I feel sure of him. Have you also been in the Service, may I ask?'

'I have,' was the reply; 'but I was too lazy, I left it early.'

'What is your reason for being tired of life?' pursued the president.

'The same, as near as I can make out,' answered the prince; 'unadulterated laziness.'

The president started. 'D—n it,' said he, 'you must have something better than that.'

'I have no more money,' added Florizel. 'That is also a vexation, without doubt. It brings my sense of idleness to an acute point.'

The president rolled his cigar round in his mouth for some seconds, directing his gaze straight into the eyes of this unusual neophyte; but the prince supported his scrutiny with unabashed good temper.

'If I had not a deal of experience,' said the president at last, 'I should turn you off. But I know the world; and this much any way, that the most frivolous excuses for a suicide are often the toughest to stand by. And when I downright like a man, as I do you, sir, I would rather strain the regulation than deny him.'

The prince and the colonel, one after the other, were subjected to a long and particular interrogatory: the prince alone; but Geraldine in the presence of the prince, so that the president might observe the countenance of the one while the other was being warmly cross-examined. The result was satisfactory; and the president, after having booked a few details of each case, produced a form of oath to be accepted. Nothing could be conceived more passive than the obedience promised, or more stringent than the terms by which the juror bound himself. The man who forfeited a pledge so awful could scarcely have a rag of honour or any of the consolations of religion left to him. Florizel signed the document, but not without a shudder; the colonel followed his example with an air of great depression. Then the president received the entry money; and without more ado, introduced the two friends into the smoking room of the Suicide Club.

The smoking room of the Suicide Club was the same height as the cabinet into which it opened, but much larger, and papered from top to bottom with an imitation of oak wainscot. A large and cheerful fire and a number of gas jets illuminated the company. The prince and his follower made the number up to eighteen. Most of the party were smoking, and drinking champagne; a feverish hilarity reigned, with sudden and rather ghastly pauses.

'Is this a full meeting?' asked the prince.

'Middling,' said the president. 'By the way,' he added, 'if you have any money, it is usual to offer some champagne. It keeps up a good spirit, and is one of my own little perquisites.'

'Hammersmith,' said Florizel, 'I may leave the champagne to you.'

And with that, he turned away and began to go round among the guests. Accustomed to play the host in the highest circles, he charmed and dominated all whom he approached; there was something at once winning and authoritative in his address; and his extraordinary coolness gave him yet another distinction in this half maniacal society. As he went from one to another, he kept both his eyes and ears open, and soon began to gain a general idea of the people among whom he found himself. As in all other places of resort, one type predominated: people in the prime of youth, with every show of intelligence and sensibility in their appearance, but with little promise of strength or the quality that makes success. Few were much above thirty, and not a few were still in their teens. They stood, leaning on tables and shifting on their feet; sometimes they smoked extraordinarily fast, and sometimes they let their cigars go out; some talked well, but the conversation of others was plainly the result of nervous tension, and was equally without wit or purport. As each new bottle of champagne was opened, there was a manifest improvement in gaiety. Only two were seated—one in a chair in the recess of the window, with his head hanging and his hands plunged deep into his trouser pockets, pale, visibly moist with perspiration, saying never a word, a very wreck of soul and body; the other sat on the divan close by the chimney, and attracted notice by a trenchant dissimilarity from all the rest. He was probably upwards of forty, but he looked fully ten years older; and Florizel thought he had never seen a man more naturally hideous, nor one more ravaged by disease and ruinous excitements. He was no more than skin and bone, was partly paralysed, and wore spectacles of such unusual power, that his eyes appeared through the glasses greatly magnified and distorted in shape. Except the prince and the president, he was the only person in the room who preserved the composure of ordinary life.

There was little decency among the members of the club. Some boasted of the disgraceful actions, the consequences of which had reduced them to seek refuge in death; and the others listened without disapproval. There was a tacit understanding against moral judgments; and whoever passed the club doors enjoyed already some of the immunities of the tomb. They drank to each other's memories, and to those of notable suicides in the past. They compared and developed their different views of death—some declaring that it was no more than blackness and cessation; others full of a hope that that very night they should be scaling the stars and commencing with the mighty dead.

'To the eternal memory of Baron Trenck, the type of suicides!' cried one. 'He went out of a small cell into a smaller, that he might come forth again to freedom.'

'For my part,' said a second, 'I wish no more than a bandage for my eyes and cotton for my ears. Only they have no cotton thick enough in this world.'

A third was for reading the mysteries of life in a future state; and a fourth professed that he would never have joined the club, if he had not been induced to believe in Mr Darwin.

'I could not bear,' said this remarkable suicide, 'to be descended from an ape.'

Altogether, the prince was disappointed by the bearing and conversation of the members.

'It does not seem to me,' he thought, 'a matter for so much disturbance. If a man has made up his mind to kill himself, let him do it, in God's name, like a gentleman. This flutter and big talk is out of place.'

In the meanwhile, Colonel Geraldine was a prey to the blackest apprehensions; the club and its rules were still a mystery, and he looked round the room for some one who should be able to set his mind at rest. In this survey his eye lighted on the paralytic person with the strong spectacles; and seeing him so exceedingly tranquil, he besought the president, who was going in and out of the room under a pressure of business, to present him to the gentleman on the divan.

The functionary explained the needlessness of all such formalities within the club, but nevertheless presented Mr Hammersmith to Mr Malthus.

Mr Malthus looked at the colonel curiously, and then requested him to take a seat upon his right.

'You are a newcomer,' he said, 'and wish information? You have come to the proper source. It is two years since I first visited this charming club.'

The colonel breathed again. If Mr Malthus had frequented the place for two years there could be little danger for the prince in a single evening. But Geraldine was none the less astonished, and began to suspect a mystification.

'What!' cried he, 'two years! I thought—but indeed I see I have been made the subject of a pleasantry.'

'By no means,' replied Mr Malthus mildly. 'My case is peculiar. I am not, properly speaking, a suicide at all; but, as it were, an honorary member. I rarely visit the club twice in two months. My infirmity and the kindness of the president have procured me these little immunities, for which besides I pay at an advanced rate. Even as it is my luck has been extraordinary.'

'I am afraid,' said the colonel, 'that I must ask you to be more explicit. You must remember that I am still most imperfectly acquainted with the rules of the club.'

'An ordinary member who comes here in search of death like yourself,' replied the paralytic, 'returns every evening until fortune favours him. He can even, if he is penniless, get board and lodging from the president: very fair, I believe, and clean, although, of course, not luxurious; that could hardly be, considering the exiguity (if I may so express myself) of the subscription. And then the president's company is a delicacy in itself.'

'Indeed!' cried Geraldine, 'he had not greatly prepossessed me.'

'Ah!' said Mr Malthus, 'you do not know the man: the drollest fellow! What stories! What cynicism! He knows life to admiration and, between ourselves, is probably the most corrupt rogue in Christendom.'

'And he also,' asked the colonel, 'is a permanency—like yourself, if I may say so without offence?'

'Indeed, he is a permanency in a very different sense from me,' replied Mr Malthus. 'I have been graciously spared, but I must go at last. Now he never plays. He shuffles and deals for the club, and makes the necessary arrangements. That man, my dear Mr Hammersmith, is the very soul of ingenuity. For three years, he has pursued in London his useful and, I think I may add, his artistic calling; and not so much as a whisper of suspicion has been once aroused. I believe him myself to be inspired. You doubtless remember the celebrated case, six months ago, of the gentleman who was accidentally poisoned in a chemist's shop? That was one of the least rich, one of the least racy, of his notions; but then, how simple! And how safe!'

'You astound me,' said the colonel. 'Was that unfortunate gentleman one of the—' He was about to say 'victims'; but bethinking himself in time, he substituted—'members of the club?'

In the same flash of thought, it occurred to him that Mr Malthus himself had not at all spoken in the tone of one who is in love with death; and he added hurriedly:

'But I perceive I am still in the dark. You speak of shuffling and dealing; pray for what end? And since you seem rather unwilling to die than otherwise, I must own that I cannot conceive what brings you here at all.'

'You say truly that you are in the dark,' replied Mr Malthus with more animation. 'Why, my dear sir, this club is the temple of intoxication. If my enfeebled health could support the excitement more often, you may depend upon it I should be more often here. It requires all the sense of duty engendered by a long habit of ill-health and careful regimen, to keep me from excess in this, which is, I may say, my last dissipation. I have tried them all, sir,' he went on, laying his hand on Geraldine's arm, 'all without exception, and I declare to you, upon my honour, there is not one of them that has not been grossly and untruthfully overrated. People trifle with love. Now, I deny that love is a strong passion. Fear is the strong passion; it is with fear that you must trifle, if you wish to taste the intensest joys of living. Envy me—envy me, sir,' he added with a chuckle, 'I am a coward!'

Geraldine could scarcely repress a movement of repulsion for this deplorable wretch; but he commanded himself with an effort, and continued his inquiries.

'How, sir,' he asked, 'is the excitement so artfully prolonged? and where is there any element of uncertainty?'

'I must tell you how the victim for every evening is selected,' returned Mr Malthus; 'and not only the victim, but another member, who is to be the instrument in the club's hands, and Death's high priest for that occasion.'

'Good God!' said the colonel, 'do they then kill each other?'

'The trouble of suicide is removed in that way,' returned Malthus with a nod.

'Merciful heavens!' ejaculated the colonel, 'and may you—may I—may the—my friend I mean—may any of us be pitched upon this evening as the slayer of another man's body and immortal spirit? Can such things be possible among men born of women? Oh! Infamy of infamies!'

He was about to rise in his horror, when he caught the

prince's eye. It was fixed upon him from across the room with a frowning and angry stare. And in a moment Geraldine recovered his composure.

'After all,' he added, 'why not? And since you say the game is interesting, vogue la galère—I follow the club!'

Mr Malthus had keenly enjoyed the colonel's amazement and disgust. He had the vanity of wickedness; and it pleased him to see another man give way to a generous movement, while he felt himself, in his entire corruption, superior to such emotions.

'You now, after your first moment of surprise,' said he, 'are in a position to appreciate the delights of our society. You can see how it combines the excitement of a gaming table, a duel, and a Roman amphitheatre. The Pagans did well enough; I cordially admire the refinement of their minds; but it has been reserved for a Christian country to attain this extreme, this quintessence, this absolute of poignancy. You will understand how vapid are all amusements to a man who has acquired a taste for this one. The game we play,' he continued, 'is one of extreme simplicity. A full pack—but I perceive you are about to see the thing in progress. Will you lend me the help of your arm? I am unfortunately paralysed.'

Indeed, just as Mr Malthus was beginning his description, another pair of folding doors was thrown open, and the whole club began to pass, not without some hurry, into the adjoining room. It was similar in every respect to the one from which it was entered, but somewhat differently furnished. The centre was occupied by a long green table, at which the president sat shuffling a pack of cards with great particularity. Even with the stick and the colonel's arm, Mr Malthus walked with so much difficulty that every one was seated before this pair and the prince, who had waited for them, entered the apartment; and, in consequence, the three took seats close together at the lower end of the board.

'It is a pack of fifty-two,' whispered Mr Malthus. 'Watch for the ace of spades, which is the sign of death, and the ace of clubs, which designates the official of the night. Happy, happy young men!' he added. 'You have good eyes, and can follow the game. Alas! I cannot tell an ace from a deuce across the table.'

And he proceeded to equip himself with a second pair of spectacles.

'I must at least watch the faces,' he explained.

The colonel rapidly informed his friend of all that he had learned from the honorary member, and of the horrible alternative that lay before them. The prince was conscious of a deadly chill and a contraction about his heart; he swallowed with difficulty, and looked from side to side like a man in a maze.

'One bold stroke,' whispered the colonel, 'and we may still escape.'

But the suggestion recalled the prince's spirits.

'Silence!' said he. 'Let me see that you can play like a gentleman for any stake, however serious.'

And he looked about him, once more to all appearance at his ease, although his heart beat thickly, and he was conscious of an unpleasant heat in his bosom. The members were all very quiet and intent; every one was pale, but none so pale as Mr Malthus. His eyes protruded; his head kept nodding involuntarily upon his spine; his hands found their way, one after the other, to his mouth, where they made clutches at his tremulous and ashen lips. It was plain that the honorary member enjoyed his membership on very startling terms.

'Attention, gentlemen!' said the president.

And he began slowly dealing the cards about the table in the reverse direction, pausing until each man had shown his card. Nearly every one hesitated; and sometimes you would see a player's fingers stumble more than once before he could turn over the momentous slip of pasteboard. As the prince's turn drew nearer, he was conscious of a growing and almost suffocating excitement; but he had somewhat of the gambler's nature, and recognized almost with astonishment, that there was a degree of pleasure in his sensations. The nine of clubs fell to his lot; the three of spades was dealt to Geraldine; and the queen of hearts to Mr Malthus, who was unable to suppress a sob of relief. The young man of the cream tarts almost immediately afterwards turned over the ace of clubs, and remained frozen with horror, the card still resting on his finger; he had not come there to kill, but to be killed; and the prince in his generous sympathy with his position almost forgot the peril that still hung over himself and his friend.

The deal was coming round again, and still Death's card had not come out. The players held their respiration, and only breathed by gasps. The prince received another club; Geraldine had a diamond; but when Mr Malthus turned up his card a horrible noise, like that of something breaking, issued from his mouth; and he rose from his seat and sat down again, with no sign of his paralysis. It was the ace of spades. The honorary member had trifled once too often with his terrors.

Conversation broke out again almost at once. The players relaxed their rigid attitudes, and began to rise from the table and stroll back by twos and threes into the smoking room. The president stretched his arms and yawned, like a man who has finished his day's work. But Mr Malthus sat in his place, with his head in his hands, and his hands upon the table, drunk and motionless—a thing stricken down.

The prince and Geraldine made their escape at once. In the cold night air their horror of what they had witnessed was redoubled.

'Alas!' cried the prince, 'to be bound by an oath in such a

matter! To allow this wholesale trade in murder to be continued with profit and impunity! If I but dared to forfeit my pledge!'

'That is impossible for your Highness,' replied the colonel, 'whose honour is the honour of Bohemia. But I dare, and may with propriety, forfeit mine.'

'Geraldine,' said the prince, 'if your honour suffers in any of the adventures into which you follow me, not only will I never pardon you, but—what I believe will much more sensibly affect you—I should never forgive myself.'

'I receive your Highness's commands,' replied the colonel. 'Shall we go from this accursed spot?'

'Yes,' said the prince. 'Call a cab in heaven's name, and let me try to forget in slumber the memory of this night's disgrace.'

But it was notable that he carefully read the name of the court before he left it.

The next morning, as soon as the prince was stirring, Colonel Geraldine brought him a daily newspaper, with the following paragraph marked:-

'MELANCHOLY ACCIDENT.—This morning, about two o'clock, Mr Bartholomew Malthus, of 16 Chepstow Place, Westbourne Grove, on his way home from a party at a friend's house, fell over the upper parapet in Trafalgar Square, fracturing his skull and breaking a leg and an arm. Death was instantaneous. Mr Malthus, accompanied by a friend, was engaged in looking for a cab at the time of the unfortunate occurrence. As Mr Malthus was paralytic, it is thought that his fall may have been occasioned by another seizure. The unhappy gentleman was well known in the most respectable circles, and his loss will be widely and deeply deplored.'

'If ever a soul went straight to hell,' said Geraldine solemnly, 'it was that paralytic man's.'

The prince buried his face in his hands, and remained silent.

'I am almost rejoiced,' continued the colonel, 'to know that he is dead. But for our young man of the cream tarts, I confess my heart bleeds.'

'Geraldine,' said the prince, raising his face, 'that unhappy lad was last night as innocent as you and I; and this morning the guilt of blood is on his soul. When I think of the president, my heart grows sick within me. I do not know how it shall be done, but I shall have that scoundrel at my mercy as there is a God in heaven. What an experience, what a lesson, was that game of cards!'

'One,' said the colonel, 'never to be repeated.'

The prince remained so long without replying, that Geraldine grew alarmed.

'You cannot mean to return,' he said. 'You have suffered too much and seen too much horror already. The duties of your high position forbid the repetition of the hazard.'

'There is much in what you say,' replied Prince Florizel, 'and I am not altogether pleased with my own determination. Alas! In the clothes of the greatest potentate, what is there but a man? I never felt my weakness more acutely than now, Geraldine, but it is stronger than I. Can I cease to interest myself in the fortunes of the unhappy young man who supped with us some hours ago? Can I leave the president to follow his nefarious career unwatched? Can I begin an adventure so entrancing, and not follow it to an end? No, Geraldine: you ask of the prince more than the man is able to perform. Tonight, once more, we take our places at the table of the Suicide Club.'

Colonel Geraldine fell upon his knees.

'Will your Highness take my life?' he cried. 'It is his—his freely; but do not, O do not! Let him ask me to countenance so terrible a risk.'

'Colonel Geraldine,' replied the prince, with some haughtiness of manner, 'your life is absolutely your own. I only looked for obedience; and when that is unwillingly rendered, I shall look for that no longer. I add one word: your importunity in this affair has been sufficient.'

The Master of the Horse regained his feet at once.

'Your Highness,' he said, 'may I be excused in my attendance this afternoon? I dare not, as an honourable man, venture a second time into that fatal house until I have perfectly ordered my affairs. Your Highness shall meet, I promise him, with no more opposition from the most devoted and grateful of his servants.'

'My dear Geraldine,' returned Prince Florizel, 'I always regret when you oblige me to remember my rank. Dispose of your day as you think fit, but be here before eleven in the same disguise.'

The club, on this second evening, was not so fully attended; and when Geraldine and the Prince arrived, there were not above half a dozen persons in the smoking room. His Highness took the President aside and congratulated him warmly on the demise of Mr Malthus.

'I like,' he said, 'to meet with capacity, and certainly find much of it in you. Your profession is of a very delicate nature, but I see you are well qualified to conduct it with success and secrecy.'

The president was somewhat affected by these compliments from one of his Highness's superior bearing. He acknowledged them almost with humility.

'Poor Malthy!' he added, 'I shall hardly know the club without him. The most of my patrons are boys, sir, and poetical boys, who are not much company for me. Not but what Malthy had some poetry, too; but it was of a kind that I could understand.'

'I can readily imagine you should find yourself in sympathy with Mr Malthus,' returned the prince. 'He struck me as a man of a very original disposition.'

The young man of the cream tarts was in the room, but painfully depressed and silent. His late companions sought in vain to lead him into conversation.

'How bitterly I wish,' he cried, 'that I had never brought you to this infamous abode! Begone, while you are clean-handed. If you could have heard the old man scream as he fell, and the noise of his bones upon the pavement! Wish me, if you have any kindness to so fallen a being—wish the ace of spades for me tonight!'

A few more members dropped in as the evening went on, but the club did not muster more than the devil's dozen when they took their places at the table. The prince was again conscious of a certain joy in his alarms; but he was astonished to see Geraldine so much more self-possessed than on the night before.

'It is extraordinary,' thought the prince, 'that a will, made or unmade, should so greatly influence a young man's spirit.'

'Attention, gentlemen!' said the president, and he began to deal.

Three times the cards went all round the table, and neither of the marked cards had yet fallen from his hand. The excitement as he began the fourth distribution was overwhelming. There were just cards enough to go once more entirely round. The prince, who sat second from the dealer's left, would receive, in the reverse mode of dealing practised at the club, the second last card. The third player turned up a black ace—it was the ace of clubs. The next received a diamond, the next a heart, and so on; but the ace of spades was still undelivered. At last, Geraldine, who sat upon the prince's left, turned his card; it was an ace, but the ace of hearts.

When Prince Florizel saw his fate upon the table in front of him, his heart stood still. He was a brave man, but the sweat poured off his face. There were exactly fifty chances out of a hundred that he was doomed. He reversed the card; it was the ace of spades. A loud roaring filled his brain, and the table swam before his eyes. He heard the player on his right break into a fit of laughter that sounded between mirth and disappointment; he saw the company rapidly dispersing, but his mind was full of other thoughts. He recognized how foolish, how criminal, had been his conduct. In perfect health, in the prime of his years, the heir to a throne, he had gambled away his future and that of a brave and loyal country. 'God,' he cried, 'God forgive me!' And with that, the confusion of his senses passed away, and he regained his self-possession in a moment.

To his surprise Geraldine had disappeared. There was no one in the card room but his destined butcher consulting with the president, and the young man of the cream tarts, who slipped up to the prince, and whispered in his ear:

'I would give a million, if I had it, for your luck.'

His Highness could not help reflecting, as the young man departed, that he would have sold his opportunity for a much more moderate sum.

The whispered conference now came to an end. The holder of the ace of clubs left the room with a look of intelligence, and the president, approaching the unfortunate prince, proffered him his hand.

'I am pleased to have met you, sir,' said he, 'and pleased to have been in a position to do you this trifling service. At least, you cannot complain of delay. On the second evening—what a stroke of luck!'

The prince endeavoured in vain to articulate something in response, but his mouth was dry and his tongue seemed paralysed.

'You feel a little sickish?' asked the president, with some show of solicitude. 'Most gentlemen do. Will you take a little brandy?'

The prince signified in the affirmative, and the other immediately filled some of the spirit into a tumbler.

'Poor old Malthy!' ejaculated the president, as the prince drained the glass. 'He drank near upon a pint, and little enough good it seemed to do him!'

'I am more amenable to treatment,' said the prince, a good deal revived. 'I am my own man again at once, as you perceive. And so, let me ask you, what are my directions?'

'You will proceed along the Strand in the direction of the city, and on the left-hand pavement, until you meet the gentleman who has just left the room. He will continue your instructions, and him you will have the kindness to obey; the authority of the club is vested in his person for the night. And now,' added the president, 'I wish you a pleasant walk.'

Florizel acknowledged the salutation rather awkwardly, and took his leave. He passed through the smoking room, where the bulk of the players were still consuming champagne, some of which he had himself ordered and paid for; and he was surprised to find himself cursing them in his heart. He put on his hat and greatcoat in the cabinet, and selected his umbrella from a corner. The familiarity of these acts, and the thought that he was about them for the last time, betrayed him into a fit of laughter which sounded unpleasantly in his own ears. He conceived a reluctance to leave the cabinet, and turned instead to the window. The sight of the lamps and the darkness recalled him to himself.

'Come, come, I must be a man,' he thought, 'and tear myself away.' At the corner of Box Court three men fell upon Prince Florizel and he was unceremoniously thrust into a carriage, which at once drove rapidly away. There was already an occupant.

'Will your Highness pardon my zeal?' said a well-known voice.

The prince threw himself upon the colonel's neck in a passion of relief.

'How can I ever thank you?' he cried. 'And how was this effected?'

Although he had been willing to march upon his doom, he was overjoyed to yield to friendly violence, and return once more to life and hope.

'You can thank me effectually enough,' replied the colonel, 'by avoiding all such dangers in the future. And as for your second question, all has been managed by the simplest means. I arranged this afternoon with a celebrated detective. Secrecy has been promised and paid for. Your own servants have been principally engaged in the affair. The house in Box Court has been surrounded since nightfall, and this, which is one of your own carriages, has been awaiting you for nearly an hour.'

'And the miserable creature who was to have slain me—what of him?' inquired the prince.

'He was pinioned as he left the club,' replied the colonel, 'and now awaits your sentence at the palace, where he will soon be joined by his accomplices.'

'Geraldine,' said the prince, 'you have saved me against my explicit orders, and you have done well. I owe you not only my life, but a lesson; and I should be unworthy of my rank if I did not show myself grateful to my teacher. Let it be yours to choose the manner.'

There was a pause, during which the carriage continued to speed through the streets, and the two men were each buried in his own reflections. The silence was broken by Colonel Geraldine.

'Your Highness,' said he, 'has by this time a considerable body of prisoners. There is at least one criminal among the number to whom justice should be dealt. Our oath forbids us all recourse to law; and discretion would forbid it equally if the oath were loosened. May I inquire your Highness's intention?'

'It is decided,' answered Florizel; 'the president must fall in duel. It only remains to choose his adversary.'

'Your Highness has permitted me to name my own recompense,' said the colonel. 'Will he permit me to ask the appointment of my brother? It is an honourable post, but I dare assure your Highness that the lad will acquit himself with credit.'

'You ask me an ungracious favour,' said the prince, 'but I must refuse you nothing.'

The Colonel kissed his hand with the greatest affection; and at that moment the carriage rolled under the archway of the prince's splendid residence.

An hour after, Florizel in his official robes, and covered with all the orders of Bohemia, received the members of the Suicide Club.

'Foolish and wicked men,' said he, 'as many of you as have been driven into this strait by the lack of fortune shall receive employment and remuneration from my officers. Those who suffer under a sense of guilt must have recourse to a higher and more generous potentate than I. I feel pity for all of you, deeper than you can imagine; tomorrow you shall tell me your stories; and as you answer more frankly, I shall be the more able to remedy your misfortunes. As for you,' he added, turning to the president, 'I should only offend a person of your parts by any offer of assistance; but I have instead a piece of diversion to propose to you. Here,' laying his hand on the shoulder of Colonel Geraldine's young brother, 'is an officer of mine who desires to make a little tour upon the continent; and I ask you, as a favour, to accompany him on this excursion. Do you,' he went on, changing his tone, 'do you shoot well with the pistol? Because you may have need of that accomplishment. When two men go travelling together, it is best to be prepared for all.

Let me add that, if by any chance you should lose young Mr Geraldine upon the way, I shall always have another member of my household to place at your disposal; and I am known, Mr President, to have long eyesight, and as long an arm.'

With these words, said with much sternness, the prince concluded his address. Next morning the members of the club were suitably provided for by his munificence, and the president set forth upon his travels, under the supervision of Mr Geraldine, and a pair of faithful and adroit lackeys, well trained in the prince's household. Not content with this, discreet agents were put in possession of the house in Box Court, and all letters or visitors for the Suicide Club or its officials were to be examined by Prince Florizel in person.

Here (says my Arabian author) ends the STORY OF THE YOUNG MAN WITH THE CREAM TARTS, who is now a comfortable householder in Wigmore Street, Cavendish Square. The number, for obvious reasons, I suppress.

2

STORY OF THE PHYSICIAN AND THE SARATOGA TRUNK

Mr Silas Q. Scuddamore was a young American of a simple and harmless disposition, which was the more to his credit as he came from New England—a quarter of the New World not precisely famous for those qualities. Although he was exceedingly rich, he kept a note of all his expenses in a little paper pocketbook; and he had chosen to study the attractions of Paris from the seventh story of what is called a furnished hotel, in the Latin Quarter. There was a great deal of habit in his penuriousness; and his virtue, which was very remarkable among his associates, was principally founded upon diffidence and youth.

The next room to his was inhabited by a lady, very attractive in her air and very elegant in toilette, whom, on his first arrival, he had taken for a countess. In course of time he had learned that she was known by the name of Madame Zephyrine, and that whatever station she occupied in life it was not that of a person of title. Madame Zephyrine, probably in the hope of enchanting the young American, used to flaunt by him on the stairs with a civil inclination, a word of course, and a knockdown look out of her black eyes, and disappear in a rustle of silk, and with the revelation of an admirable foot and ankle.

But these advances, so far from encouraging Mr Scuddamore, plunged him into the depths of depression and bashfulness. She had come to him several times for a light, or to apologize for the imaginary depredations of her poodle; but his mouth was closed in the presence of so superior a being, his French promptly left him, and he could only stare and stammer until she was gone. The slenderness of their intercourse did not prevent him from throwing out insinuations of a very glorious order when he was safely alone with a few males.

The room on the other side of the American's—for there were three rooms on a floor in the hotel—was tenanted by an old English physician of rather doubtful reputation. Dr. Noel, for that was his name, had been forced to leave London, where he enjoyed a large and increasing practice; and it was hinted that the police had been the instigators of this change of scene. At least he, who had made something of a figure in earlier life, now dwelt in the Latin Quarter in great simplicity and solitude, and devoted much of his time to study. Mr Scuddamore had made his acquaintance, and the pair would now and then dine together frugally in a restaurant across the street.

Silas Q. Scuddamore had many little vices of the more respectable order, and was not restrained by delicacy from indulging them in many rather doubtful ways. Chief among his foibles stood curiosity. He was a born gossip; and life, and especially those parts of it in which he had no experience, interested him to the degree of passion. He was a pert, invincible questioner, pushing his inquiries with equal pertinacity and indiscretion; he had been observed, when he took a letter to the post, to weigh it in his hand, to turn it over and over, and to study the address with care; and when he found a flaw in the partition between his room and Madame Zephyrine's, instead of filling it up, he enlarged and improved the opening, and made use of it as a spyhole on his neighbour's affairs.

One day, in the end of March, his curiosity growing as it was indulged, he enlarged the hole a little further, so that he might command another corner of the room. That evening, when he went as usual to inspect Madame Zephyrine's movements, he was astonished to find the aperture obscured in an odd manner on the other side, and still more abashed when the obstacle was suddenly withdrawn and a titter of laughter reached his ears. Some of the plaster had evidently betrayed the secret of his spyhole, and his neighbour had been returning the compliment in kind. Mr Scuddamore was moved to a very acute feeling of annoyance; he condemned Madame Zephyrine unmercifully; he even blamed himself; but when he found, next day, that she had taken no means to baulk him of his favourite pastime, he continued to profit by her carelessness, and gratify his idle curiosity.

That next day Madame Zephyrine received a long visit from a tall, loosely-built man of fifty or upwards, whom Silas had not hitherto seen. His tweed suit and coloured shirt, no less than his shaggy sidewhiskers, identified him as a Britisher, and his dull grey eye affected Silas with a sense of cold. He kept screwing his mouth from side to side and round and round during the whole colloquy, which was carried on in whispers. More than once it seemed to the young New Englander as if their gestures indicated his own apartment; but the only thing definite he could gather, by the most scrupulous attention, was this remark made by the Englishman in a somewhat higher key, as if in answer to some reluctance or opposition.

'I have studied his taste to a nicety, and I tell you again and again you are the only woman of the sort that I can lay my hands on.'

In answer to this, Madame Zephyrine sighed, and appeared by a gesture to resign herself, like one yielding to unqualified authority.

That afternoon, the observatory was finally blinded, a wardrobe having been drawn in front of it upon the other side; and while Silas was still lamenting over this misfortune, which he attributed to the Britisher's malign suggestion, the concierge brought him up a letter in a female handwriting. It was conceived in French of no very rigorous orthography, bore no signature, and in the most encouraging terms invited the young American to be present in a certain part of the Bullier Ball at eleven o'clock that night. Curiosity and timidity fought a long battle in his heart; sometimes he was all virtue, sometimes all fire and daring; and the result of it was that, long before ten, Mr Silas Q. Scuddamore presented himself in unimpeachable attire at the door of the Bullier Ball Rooms, and paid his entry money with a sense of reckless devilry that was not without its charm.

It was carnival time, and the ball was very full and noisy. The lights and the crowd at first rather abashed our young adventurer, and then, mounting to his brain with a sort of intoxication, put him in possession of more than his own share of manhood. He felt ready to face the devil, and strutted in the ballroom with the swagger of a cavalier. While he was thus parading, he became aware of Madame Zephyrine and her Britisher in conference behind a pillar. The cat-like spirit of eaves-dropping overcame him at once. He stole nearer and nearer on the couple from behind, until he was within earshot.

'That is the man,' the Britisher was saying; 'there—with the long blond hair—speaking to a girl in green.'

Silas identified a very handsome young fellow of small stature, who was plainly the object of this designation.

'It is well,' said Madame Zephyrine. 'I shall do my utmost. But, remember, the best of us may fail in such a matter.'

'Tut!' returned her companion; 'I answer for the result. Have I not chosen you from thirty? Go; but be wary of the prince. I cannot think what cursed accident has brought him here tonight. As if there were not a dozen balls in Paris better worth his notice than this riot of students and counter-jumpers! See him where he sits, more like a reigning emperor at home than a prince upon his holidays!'

Silas was again lucky. He observed a person of rather a full build, strikingly handsome, and of a very stately and courteous demeanour, seated at table with another handsome young man, several years his junior, who addressed him with conspicuous deference. The name of prince struck gratefully on Silas's Republican hearing, and the aspect of the person to whom that name was applied exercised its usual charm upon his mind. He left Madame Zephyrine and her Englishman to take care of each other, and threading his way through the assembly, approached the table which the prince and his confidant had honoured with their choice.

'I tell you, Geraldine,' the former was saying, 'the action is madness. Yourself (I am glad to remember it) chose your brother for this perilous service, and you are bound in duty to have a guard upon his conduct. He has consented to delay so many days in Paris; that was already an imprudence, considering the character of the man he has to deal with; but now, when he is within eight-and-forty hours of his departure, when he is within two or three days of the decisive trial, I ask you, is this a place for him to spend his time? He should be in a gallery at practice; he should be sleeping long hours and taking moderate exercise on foot; he should be on a rigorous diet, without white wines or brandy. Does the dog imagine we are all playing comedy? The thing is deadly earnest, Geraldine.'

'I know the lad too well to interfere,' replied Colonel Geraldine, 'and well enough not to be alarmed. He is more cautious than you fancy, and of an indomitable spirit. If it had been a woman I should not say so much, but I trust the president to him and the two valets without an instant's apprehension.'

'I am gratified to hear you say so,' replied the prince; 'but my mind is not at rest. These servants are well-trained spies, and already has not this miscreant succeeded three times in eluding their observation and spending several hours on end in private, and most likely dangerous, affairs? An amateur might have lost him by accident, but if Rudolph and Jerome were thrown off the scent, it must have been done on purpose, and by a man who had a cogent reason and exceptional resources.'

'I believe the question is now one between my brother and myself,' replied Geraldine, with a shade of offence in his tone.

'I permit it to be so, Colonel Geraldine,' returned Prince Florizel. 'Perhaps, for that very reason, you should be all the more ready to accept my counsels. But enough. That girl in yellow dances well.'

And the talk veered into the ordinary topics of a Paris ballroom in the carnival.

Silas remembered where he was, and that the hour was already near at hand when he ought to be upon the scene of his assignation. The more he reflected the less he liked the prospect, and as at that moment an eddy in the crowd began to draw him in the direction of the door, he suffered it to carry him away without resistance. The eddy stranded him in a corner under the gallery, where his ear was immediately struck with the voice of Madame Zephyrine. She was speaking in French with the young man of the blond locks who had been pointed out by the strange Britisher not half an hour before.

'I have a character at stake,' she said, 'or I would put no other condition than my heart recommends. But you have only to say so much to the porter, and he will let you go by without a word.'

'But why this talk of debt?' objected her companion.

'Heavens!' said she, 'do you think I do not understand my

own hotel?'

And she went by, clinging affectionately to her companion's arm.

This put Silas in mind of his billet.

'Ten minutes hence,' thought he, 'and I may be walking with as beautiful a woman as that, and even better dressed—perhaps a real lady, possibly a woman or title.'

And then he remembered the spelling, and was a little downcast.

'But it may have been written by her maid,' he imagined.

The clock was only a few minutes from the hour, and this immediate proximity set his heart beating at a curious and rather disagreeable speed. He reflected with relief that he was in no way bound to put in an appearance. Virtue and cowardice were together, and he made once more for the door, but this time of his own accord, and battling against the stream of people which was now moving in a contrary direction. Perhaps this prolonged resistance wearied him, or perhaps he was in that frame of mind when merely to continue in the same determination for a certain number of minutes produces a reaction and a different purpose. Certainly, at least, he wheeled about for a third time, and did not stop until he had found a place of concealment within a few yards of the appointed place.

Here he went through an agony of spirit, in which he several times prayed to God for help, for Silas had been devoutly educated. He had now not the least inclination for the meeting; nothing kept him from flight but a silly fear lest he should be thought unmanly; but this was so powerful that it kept head against all other motives; and although it could not decide him to advance, prevented him from definitely running away. At last the clock indicated ten minutes past the hour. Young Scuddamore's spirit began to rise; he peered round the corner and saw no one at the place of meeting; doubtless his unknown correspondent had wearied and gone away. He became as bold as he had formerly been timid. It seemed to him that if he came at all to the appointment, however late, he was clear from the charge of cowardice. Nay, now he began to suspect a hoax, and actually complimented himself on his shrewdness in having suspected and outmanoeuvred his mystifiers. So very idle a thing is a boy's mind!

Armed with these reflections, he advanced boldly from his corner; but he had not taken above a couple of steps before a hand was laid upon his arm. He turned and beheld a lady cast in a very large mould and with somewhat stately features, but bearing no mark of severity in her looks.

'I see that you are a very self-confident ladykiller,' said she; 'for you make yourself expected. But I was determined to meet you. When a woman has once so far forgotten herself as to make the first advance, she has long ago left behind her all considerations of petty pride.'

Silas was overwhelmed by the size and attractions of his correspondent and the suddenness with which she had fallen upon him. But she soon set him at his ease. She was very towardly and lenient in her behaviour; she led him on to make pleasantries, and then applauded him to the echo; and in a very short time, between blandishments and a liberal exhibition of warm brandy, she had not only induced him to fancy himself in love, but to declare his passion with the greatest vehemence.

'Alas!' she said; 'I do not know whether I ought not to deplore this moment, great as is the pleasure you give me by your words. Hitherto I was alone to suffer; now, poor boy, there will be two. I am not my own mistress. I dare not ask you to visit me at my own house, for I am watched by jealous eyes. Let me see,' she added; 'I am older than you, although so much weaker; and while I trust in your courage and determination, I must employ my own knowledge of the world for our mutual benefit. Where do you live?'

He told her that he lodged in a furnished hotel, and named the street and number.

She seemed to reflect for some minutes, with an effort of mind.

'I see,' she said at last. 'You will be faithful and obedient, will you not?'

Silas assured her eagerly of his fidelity.

'Tomorrow night, then,' she continued, with an encouraging smile, 'you must remain at home all the evening; and if any friends should visit you, dismiss them at once on any pretext that most readily presents itself. Your door is probably shut by ten?' she asked.

'By eleven,' answered Silas.

'At a quarter past eleven,' pursued the lady, 'leave the house. Merely cry for the door to be opened, and be sure you fall into no talk with the porter, as that might ruin everything. Go straight to the corner where the Luxembourg Gardens join the Boulevard; there you will find me waiting you. I trust you to follow my advice from point to point: and remember, if you fail me in only one particular, you will bring the sharpest trouble on a woman whose only fault is to have seen and loved you.'

'I cannot see the use of all these instructions,' said Silas.

'I believe you are already beginning to treat me as a master,' she cried, tapping him with her fan upon the arm. 'Patience, patience! That should come in time. A woman loves to be obeyed at first, although afterwards she finds her pleasure in obeying. Do as I ask you, for heaven's sake, or I will answer for nothing. Indeed, now I think of it,' she added, with the manner of one who has just seen further into a difficulty, 'I find a better plan of keeping importunate visitors away. Tell the porter to admit no one for you, except a person who may come that night to claim a debt; and speak with some feeling, as though you feared the interview, so that he may take your words in earnest.'

'I think you may trust me to protect myself against intruders,' he said, not without a little pique.

'That is how I should prefer the thing arranged,' she answered coldly. 'I know you men; you think nothing of a woman's reputation.'

Silas blushed and somewhat hung his head; for the scheme he had in view had involved a little vaingloriying before his acquaintances.

'Above all,' she added, 'do not speak to the porter as you come out.'

'And why?' said he. 'Of all your instructions, that seems to me the least important.'

'You at first doubted the wisdom of some of the others, which you now see to be very necessary,' she replied. 'Believe me, this also has its uses; in time you will see them; and what am I to think of your affection, if you refuse me such trifles at our first interview?'

Silas confounded himself in explanations and apologies; in the middle of these she looked up at the clock and clapped her hands together with a suppressed scream.

'Heavens!' she cried, 'is it so late? I have not an instant to lose. Alas, we poor women, what slaves we are! What have I not risked for you already?'

And after repeating her directions, which she artfully combined with caresses and the most abandoned looks, she bade him farewell and disappeared among the crowd.

The whole of the next day Silas was filled with a sense of great importance; he was now sure she was a countess; and when evening came he minutely obeyed her orders and was at the corner of the Luxembourg Gardens by the hour appointed. No one was there. He waited nearly half an hour, looking in the face of every one who passed or loitered near the spot; he even visited the neighbouring corners of the Boulevard and made a complete circuit of the garden railings; but there was no beautiful countess to throw herself into his arms. At last, and most reluctantly, he began to retrace his steps towards his hotel. On the way he remembered the words he had heard pass between Madame Zephyrine and the blond young man, and they gave him an indefinite uneasiness.

'It appears,' he reflected, 'that every one has to tell lies to our porter.'

He rang the bell, the door opened before him, and the porter in his bed clothes came to offer him a light.

'Has he gone?' inquired the porter.

'He? Whom do you mean?' asked Silas, somewhat sharply, for he was irritated by his disappointment.

'I did not notice him go out,' continued the porter, 'but I trust you paid him. We do not care, in this house, to have lodgers who cannot meet their liabilities.'

'What the devil do you mean?' demanded Silas rudely. 'I cannot understand a word of this farrago.'

'The short blond young man who came for his debt,' returned the other. 'Him it is I mean. Who else should it be, when I had your orders to admit no one else?'

'Why, good God, of course he never came,' retorted Silas.

'I believe what I believe,' returned the porter, putting his tongue into his cheek with a most roguish air.

'You are an insolent scoundrel,' cried Silas, and, feeling that he had made a ridiculous exhibition of asperity, and at the same time bewildered by a dozen alarms, he turned and began to run upstairs.

'Do you not want a light then?' cried the porter.

But Silas only hurried the faster, and did not pause until he had reached the seventh landing and stood in front of his own door. There he waited a moment to recover his breath, assailed by the worst forebodings and almost dreading to enter the room.

When at last he did so he was relieved to find it dark, and to all appearance, untenanted. He drew a long breath. Here he was, home again in safety, and this should be his last folly as certainly as it had been his first. The matches stood on a little table by the bed, and he began to grope his way in that direction. As he moved, his apprehensions grew upon him once more, and he was pleased, when his foot encountered an obstacle, to find it nothing more alarming than a chair. At last he touched curtains. From the position of the window, which was faintly visible, he knew he must be at the foot of the bed, and had only to feel his way along it in order to reach the table in question.

He lowered his hand, but what it touched was not simply a counterpane—it was a counterpane with something underneath it like the outline of a human leg. Silas withdrew his arm and stood a moment petrified.

'What, what,' he thought, 'can this betoken?'

He listened intently, but there was no sound of breathing. Once more, with a great effort, he reached out the end of his finger to the spot he had already touched; but this time he leaped back half a yard, and stood shivering and fixed with terror. There was something in his bed. What it was he knew not, but there was something there.

It was some seconds before he could move. Then, guided by an instinct, he fell straight upon the matches, and keeping his back towards the bed lighted a candle. As soon as the flame had kindled, he turned slowly round and looked for what he feared to see. Sure enough, there was the worst of his imaginations realized. The coverlid was drawn carefully up over the pillow, but it moulded the outline of a human body lying motionless;

and when he dashed forward and flung aside the sheets, he beheld the blond young man whom he had seen in the Bullier Ball the night before, his eyes open and without speculation, his face swollen and blackened, and a thin stream of blood trickling from his nostrils.

Silas uttered a long, tremulous wail, dropped the candle, and fell on his knees beside the bed.

Silas was awakened from the stupor into which his terrible discovery had plunged him by a prolonged but discreet tapping at the door. It took him some seconds to remember his position; and when he hastened to prevent anyone from entering it was already too late. Dr Noel, in a tall night-cap, carrying a lamp which lighted up his long white countenance, sidling in his gait, and peering and cocking his head like some sort of bird, pushed the door slowly open, and advanced into the middle of the room.

'I thought I heard a cry,' began the doctor, 'and fearing you might be unwell I did not hesitate to offer this intrusion.'

Silas, with a flushed face and a fearful beating heart, kept between the doctor and the bed; but he found no voice to answer.

'You are in the dark,' pursued the doctor; 'and yet you have not even begun to prepare for rest. You will not easily persuade me against my own eyesight; and your face declares most eloquently that you require either a friend or a physician—which is it to be? Let me feel your pulse, for that is often a just reporter of the heart.'

He advanced to Silas, who still retreated before him backwards, and sought to take him by the wrist; but the strain on the young American's nerves had become too great for endurance. He avoided the doctor with a febrile movement, and, throwing himself upon the floor, burst into a flood of weeping.

As soon as Dr Noel perceived the dead man in the bed his face darkened; and hurrying back to the door which he had left ajar, he hastily closed and double-locked it.

'Up!' he cried, addressing Silas in strident tones; 'this is no time for weeping. What have you done? How came this body in your room? Speak freely to one who may be helpful. Do you imagine I would ruin you? Do you think this piece of dead flesh on your pillow can alter in any degree the sympathy with which you have inspired me? Credulous youth, the horror with which blind and unjust law regards an action never attaches to the doer in the eyes of those who love him; and if I saw the friend of my heart return to me out of seas of blood he would be in no way changed in my affection. Raise yourself,' he said; 'good and ill are a chimera; there is nought in life except destiny, and however you may be circumstanced there is one at your side who will help you to the last.'

Thus encouraged, Silas gathered himself together, and in a broken voice, and helped out by the doctor's interrogations, contrived at last to put him in possession of the facts. But the conversation between the prince and Geraldine he altogether omitted, as he had understood little of its purport, and had no idea that it was in any way related to his own misadventure.

'Alas!' cried Dr Noel, 'I am much abused, or you have fallen innocently into the most dangerous hands in Europe. Poor boy, what a pit has been dug for your simplicity! Into what a deadly peril have your unwary feet been conducted! This man,' he said, 'this Englishman, whom you twice saw, and whom I suspect to be the soul of the contrivance, can you describe him? Was he young or old? Tall or short?'

But Silas, who, for all his curiosity, had not a seeing eye in his head, was able to supply nothing but meagre generalities, which it was impossible to recognize.

'I would have it a piece of education in all schools!' cried the doctor angrily. 'Where is the use of eyesight and articulate speech if a man cannot observe and recollect the features of his enemy? I, who know all the gangs of Europe, might have identified him, and gained new weapons for your defence. Cultivate this art in future, my poor boy; you may find it of momentous service.'

'The future!' repeated Silas. 'What future is there left for me except the gallows?'

'Youth is but a cowardly season,' returned the doctor; 'and a man's own troubles look blacker than they are. I am old, and yet I never despair.'

'Can I tell such a story to the police?' demanded Silas.

'Assuredly not,' replied the doctor. 'From what I see already of the machination in which you have been involved, your case is desperate upon that side; and for the narrow eye of the authorities you are infallibly the guilty person. And remember that we only know a portion of the plot; and the same infamous contrivers have doubtless arranged many other circumstances which would be elicited by a police inquiry, and help to fix the guilt more certainly upon your innocence.'

'I am then lost, indeed!' cried Silas.

'I have not said so,' answered Dr Noel, 'for I am a cautious man.'

'But look at this!' objected Silas, pointing to the body. 'Here is this object in my bed; not to be explained, not to be disposed of, not to be regarded without horror.'

'Horror?' replied the doctor. 'No. When this sort of clock has run down, it is no more to me than an ingenious piece of mechanism, to be investigated with the bistoury. When blood is once cold and stagnant, it is no longer human blood; when flesh is once dead, it is no longer that flesh which we desire in our lovers and respect in our friends. The grace, the attraction, the terror, have all gone from it with the animating spirit. Accustom yourself to look upon it with composure; for if my scheme is practicable you will have to live some days in constant proximity to that which now so greatly horrifies you.'

'Your scheme?' cried Silas. 'What is that? Tell me speedily, doctor; for I have scarcely courage enough to continue to exist.'

Without replying, Doctor Noel turned towards the bed, and proceeded to examine the corpse.

'Quite dead,' he murmured. 'Yes, as I had supposed, the pockets empty. Yes, and the name cut off the shirt. Their work has been done thoroughly and well. Fortunately, he is of small stature.'

Silas followed these words with an extreme anxiety. At last the doctor, his autopsy completed, took a chair and addressed the young American with a smile.

'Since I came into your room,' said he, 'although my ears and my tongue have been so busy, I have not suffered my eyes to remain idle. I noted a little while ago that you have there, in the corner, one of those monstrous constructions which your fellow-countrymen carry with them into all quarters of the globe—in a word, a Saratoga trunk. Until this moment I have never been able to conceive the utility of these erections; but then I began to have a glimmer. Whether it was for convenience in the slave trade, or to obviate the results of too ready an employment of the bowie knife, I cannot bring myself to decide. But one thing I see plainly—the object of such a box is to contain a human body.'

'Surely,' cried Silas, 'surely this is not a time for jesting.'

'Although I may express myself with some degree of pleasantry,' replied the doctor, 'the purport of my words is entirely serious. And the first thing we have to do, my young friend, is to empty your coffer of all that it contains.'

Silas, obeying the authority of Doctor Noel, put himself at his disposition. The Saratoga trunk was soon gutted of its contents, which made a considerable litter on the floor; and then—Silas taking the heels and the doctor supporting the shoulders—the body of the murdered man was carried from the bed, and, after some difficulty, doubled up and inserted whole into the empty box. With an effort on the part of both, the lid was forced down upon this unusual baggage, and the trunk was locked and corded by the doctor's own hand, while Silas disposed of what had been taken out between the closet and a chest of drawers.

'Now,' said the doctor, 'the first step has been taken on the way to your deliverance. Tomorrow, or rather today, it must be your task to allay the suspicions of your porter, paying him all that you owe; while you may trust me to make the arrangements necessary to a safe conclusion. Meantime, follow me to my room, where I shall give you a safe and powerful opiate; for, whatever you do, you must have rest.'

The next day was the longest in Silas's memory; it seemed as if it would never be done. He denied himself to his friends, and sat in a corner with his eyes fixed upon the Saratoga trunk in dismal contemplation. His own former indiscretions were now returned upon him in kind; for the observatory had been once more opened, and he was conscious of an almost continual study from Madame Zephyrine's apartment. So distressing did this become, that he was at last obliged to block up the spy-hole from his own side; and when he was thus secured from observation, he spent a considerable portion of his time in contrite tears and prayer.

Late in the evening Dr Noel entered the room carrying in his hand a pair of sealed envelopes without address, one somewhat bulky, and the other so slim as to seem without enclosure.

'Silas,' he said, seating himself at the table, 'the time has now come for me to explain my plan for your salvation. Tomorrow morning, at an early hour, Prince Florizel of Bohemia returns to London, after having diverted himself for a few days with the Parisian Carnival. It was my fortune, a good while ago, to do Colonel Geraldine, his Master of the Horse, one of those services, so common in my profession, which are never forgotten upon either side. I have no need to explain to you the nature of the obligation under which he was laid; suffice it to say that I knew him ready to serve me in any practicable manner. Now, it was necessary for you to gain London with your trunk unopened. To this, the Custom House seemed to oppose a fatal difficulty; but I bethought me that the baggage of so considerable a person as the prince, is, as a matter of courtesy, passed without examination by the officers of Custom. I applied to Colonel Geraldine, and succeeded in obtaining a favourable answer. Tomorrow, if you go before six to the hotel where the prince lodges, your baggage will be passed over as a part of his, and you yourself will make the journey as a member of his suite.'

'It seems to me, as you speak, that I have already seen both the prince and Colonel Geraldine; I even overheard some of their conversation the other evening at the Bullier Ball.'

'It is probable enough; for the prince loves to mix with all societies,' replied the doctor. 'Once arrived in London,' he pursued, 'your task is nearly ended. In this more bulky envelope I have given you a letter which I dare not address; but in the other you will find the designation of the house to which you must carry it along with your box, which will there be taken from you and not trouble you any more.'

'Alas!' said Silas, 'I have every wish to believe you; but how is it possible? You open up to me a bright prospect, but, I ask you, is my mind capable of receiving so unlikely a solution? Be more generous, and let me further understand your meaning.'

The doctor seemed painfully impressed.

'Boy,' he answered, 'you do not know how hard a thing you ask of me. But be it so. I am now inured to humiliation; and it would be strange if I refused you this, after having granted you so much. Know, then, that although I now make so quiet an appearance—frugal, solitary, addicted to study—when I was younger, my name was once a rallying cry among the most astute and dangerous spirits of London; and while I was outwardly an object for respect and consideration, my true power resided in the most secret, terrible, and criminal relations. It is to one of the persons who then obeyed me that I now address myself to deliver you from your burden. They were men of many different nations and dexterities, all bound together by a formidable oath, and working to the same purposes; the trade of the association was in murder; and I who speak to you, innocent as I appear, was the chieftain of this redoubtable crew.'

'What?' cried Silas. 'A murderer? And one with whom murder was a trade? Can I take your hand? Ought I so much as to accept your services? Dark and criminal old man, would you make an accomplice of my youth and my distress?'

The doctor bitterly laughed.

'You are difficult to please, Mr Scuddamore,' said he; 'but I now offer you your choice of company between the murdered man and the murderer. If your conscience is too nice to accept my aid, say so, and I will immediately leave you. Thenceforward you can deal with your trunk and its belongings as best suits your upright conscience.'

'I own myself wrong,' replied Silas. 'I should have remembered how generously you offered to shield me, even before I had convinced you of my innocence, and I continue to listen to your counsels with gratitude.'

'That is well,' returned the doctor; 'and I perceive you are beginning to learn some of the lessons of experience.'

'At the same time,' resumed the New Englander, 'as you confess yourself accustomed to this tragical business, and the people to whom you recommend me are your own former associates and friends, could you not yourself undertake the transport of the box, and rid me at once of its detested presence?'

'Upon my word,' replied the doctor, 'I admire you cordially. If you do not think I have already meddled sufficiently in your concerns, believe me, from my heart I think the contrary. Take or leave my services as I offer them; and trouble me with no more words of gratitude, for I value your consideration even more lightly than I do your intellect. A time will come, if you should be spared to see a number of years in health of mind, when you will think differently of all this, and blush for your tonight's behaviour.'

So saying, the doctor arose from his chair, repeated his directions briefly and clearly, and departed from the room without permitting Silas any time to answer.

The next morning, Silas presented himself at the hotel, where he was politely received by Colonel Geraldine, and relieved, from that moment, of all immediate alarm about his trunk and its grisly contents. The journey passed over without much incident, although the young man was horrified to overhear the sailors and railway porters complaining among themselves about the unusual weight of the prince's baggage. Silas travelled in a carriage with the valets, for Prince Florizel chose to be alone with his Master of the Horse. On board the steamer, however, Silas attracted his Highness's attention by the melancholy of his air and attitude as he stood gazing at the pile of baggage; for he was still full of disquietude about the future.

'There is a young man,' observed the prince, 'who must have some cause for sorrow.'

'That,' replied Geraldine, 'is the American for whom I obtained permission to travel with your suite.'

'You remind me that I have been remiss in courtesy,' said Prince Florizel, and advancing to Silas, he addressed him with the most exquisite condescension in these words:- 'I was charmed, young sir, to be able to gratify the desire you made known to me through Colonel Geraldine. Remember, if you please, that I shall be glad at any future time to lay you under a more serious obligation.'

And he then put some questions as to the political condition of America, which Silas answered with sense and propriety.

'You are still a young man,' said the prince; 'but I observe you to be very serious for your years. Perhaps you allow your attention to be too much occupied with grave studies. But, perhaps, on the other hand, I am myself indiscreet and touch upon a painful subject.'

'I have certainly cause to be the most miserable of men,' said Silas; 'never has a more innocent person been more dismally abused.'

'I will not ask you for your confidence,' returned Prince Florizel. 'But do not forget that Colonel Geraldine's recommendation is an unfailing passport; and that I am not only willing, but possibly more able than many others, to do you a service.'

Silas was delighted with the amiability of this great personage; but his mind soon returned upon its gloomy preoccupations; for not even the favour of a prince to a Republican can discharge a brooding spirit of its cares.

The train arrived at Charing Cross, where the officers of the Revenue respected the baggage of Prince Florizel in the usual manner. The most elegant equipages were in waiting; and Silas was driven, along with the rest, to the prince's residence. There Colonel Geraldine sought him out, and expressed himself pleased to have been of any service to a friend of the physician's, for whom he professed a great consideration.

'I hope,' he added, 'that you will find none of your porcelain injured. Special orders were given along the line to deal tenderly with the prince's effects.'

And then, directing the servants to place one of the carriages at the young gentleman's disposal, and at once to charge the Saratoga trunk upon the dickey, the colonel shook hands and excused himself on account of his occupations in the princely household.

Silas now broke the seal of the envelope containing the address, and directed the stately footman to drive him to Box Court, opening off the Strand. It seemed as if the place were not at all unknown to the man, for he looked startled and begged a repetition of the order. It was with a heart full of alarms, that Silas mounted into the luxurious vehicle, and was driven to his destination. The entrance to Box Court was too narrow for the passage of a coach; it was a mere footway between railings, with a post at either end. On one of these posts was seated a man, who at once jumped down and exchanged a friendly sign with the driver, while the footman opened the door and inquired of Silas whether he should take down the Saratoga trunk, and to what number it should be carried.

'If you please,' said Silas. 'To number three.'

The footman and the man who had been sitting on the post, even with the aid of Silas himself, had hard work to carry in the trunk; and before it was deposited at the door of the house in question, the young American was horrified to find a score of loiterers looking on. But he knocked with as good a countenance as he could muster up, and presented the other envelope to him who opened.

'He is not at home,' said he, 'but if you will leave your letter and return tomorrow early, I shall be able to inform you whether and when he can receive your visit. Would you like to leave your box?' he added.

'Dearly,' cried Silas; and the next moment he repented his precipitation, and declared, with equal emphasis, that he would rather carry the box along with him to the hotel.

The crowd jeered at his indecision and followed him to the carriage with insulting remarks; and Silas, covered with shame and terror, implored the servants to conduct him to some quiet and comfortable house of entertainment in the immediate neighbourhood.

The prince's equipage deposited Silas at the Craven Hotel in Craven Street, and immediately drove away, leaving him alone with the servants of the inn. The only vacant room, it appeared, was a little den up four pairs of stairs, and looking towards the back. To this hermitage, with infinite trouble and complaint, a pair of stout porters carried the Saratoga trunk. It is needless to mention that Silas kept closely at their heels throughout the ascent, and had his heart in his mouth at every corner. A single false step, he reflected, and the box might go over the banisters and land its fatal contents, plainly discovered, on the pavement of the hall.

Arrived in the room, he sat down on the edge of his bed to recover from the agony that he had just endured; but he had hardly taken his position when he was recalled to a sense of his peril by the action of the boots, who had knelt beside the trunk, and was proceeding officiously to undo its elaborate fastenings.

'Let it be!' cried Silas. 'I shall want nothing from it while I stay here.'

'You might have let it lie in the hall, then,' growled the man; 'a thing as big and heavy as a church. What you have inside I cannot fancy. If it is all money, you are a richer man than me.'

'Money?' repeated Silas, in a sudden perturbation. 'What do you mean by money? I have no money, and you are speaking like a fool.'

'All right, captain,' retorted the boots with a wink. 'There's nobody will touch your lordship's money. I'm as safe as the bank,' he added; 'but as the box is heavy, I shouldn't mind drinking something to your lordship's health.'

Silas pressed two Napoleons upon his acceptance, apologizing, at the same time, for being obliged to trouble him with foreign money, and pleading his recent arrival for excuse. And the man, grumbling with even greater fervour, and looking contemptuously from the money in his hand to the Saratoga trunk, and back again from the one to the other, at last consented to withdraw.

For nearly two days the dead body had been packed into Silas' box; and as soon as he was alone the unfortunate New Englander nosed all the cracks and openings with the most passionate attention. But the weather was cool, and the trunk still managed to contain his shocking secret.

He took a chair beside it, and buried his face in his hands, and his mind in the most profound reflection. If he were not speedily relieved, no question but he must be speedily discovered. Alone in a strange city, without friends or accomplices, if the doctor's introduction failed him, he was indubitably a lost New Englander. He reflected pathetically over his ambitious designs for the future; he should not now become the hero and spokesman of his native place of Bangor, Maine; he should not, as he had fondly anticipated, move on from office to office, from honour to honour; he might as well divest himself at once of all hope of being acclaimed President of the United States, and leaving behind him a statue, in the worst possible style of art, to adorn the Capitol at Washington. Here he was, chained to a dead Englishman doubled up inside a Saratoga trunk; whom he must get rid of, or perish from the rolls of national glory!

I should be afraid to chronicle the language employed by this young man to the doctor, to the murdered man, to

Madame Zephyrine, to the boots of the hotel, to the prince's servants, and, in a word, to all who had been ever so remotely connected with his horrible misfortune.

He slunk down to dinner about seven at night; but the yellow coffee room appalled him, the eyes of the other diners seemed to rest on his with suspicion, and his mind remained upstairs with the Saratoga trunk. When the waiter came to offer him cheese, his nerves were already so much on edge that he leaped halfway out of his chair and upset the remainder of a pint of ale upon the tablecloth.

The fellow offered to show him to the smoking-room when he had done; and although he would have much preferred to return at once to his perilous treasure, he had not the courage to refuse, and was shown downstairs to the black, gas-lit cellar, which formed, and possibly still forms, the divan of the Craven Hotel.

Two very sad betting men were playing billiards, attended by a moist, consumptive marker; and for the moment Silas imagined that these were the only occupants of the apartment. But at the next glance his eye fell upon a person smoking in the farthest corner, with lowered eyes and a most respectable and modest aspect. He knew at once that he had seen the face before; and, in spite of the entire change of clothes, recognized the man whom he had found seated on a post at the entrance to Box Court, and who had helped him to carry the trunk to and from the carriage. The New Englander simply turned and ran, nor did he pause until he had locked and bolted himself into his bedroom.

There, all night long, a prey to the most terrible imaginations, he watched beside the fatal boxful of dead flesh. The suggestion of the boots, that his trunk was full of gold, inspired him with all manner of new terrors, if he so much as dared to close an eye; and the presence in the smoking room, and under an obvious disguise, of the loiterer from Box Court convinced him that he was once more the centre of obscure machinations.

Midnight had sounded some time, when, impelled by uneasy suspicions, Silas opened his bedroom door and peered into the passage. It was dimly illuminated by a single jet of gas; and some distance off, he perceived a man sleeping on the floor in the costume of an hotel under-servant. Silas drew near the man on tiptoe. He lay partly on his back, partly on his side, and his right forearm concealed his face from recognition. Suddenly, while the American was still bending over him, the sleeper removed his arm and opened his eyes, and Silas found himself once more face to face with the loiterer of Box Court.

'Good-night, sir,' said the man, pleasantly.

But Silas was too profoundly moved to find an answer, and regained his room in silence.

Towards morning, worn out by apprehension, he fell asleep on his chair, with his head forward on the trunk. In spite of so constrained an attitude and such a grisly pillow, his slumber was sound and prolonged, and he was only awakened at a late hour and by a sharp tapping at the door.

He hurried to open, and found the boots without.

'You are the gentleman who called yesterday at Box Court?' he asked.

Silas, with a quaver, admitted that he had done so.

'Then this note is for you,' added the servant, proffering a sealed envelope.

Silas tore it open, and found inside the words: 'Twelve o'clock.'

He was punctual to the hour; the trunk was carried before him by several stout servants; and he was himself ushered into a room, where a man sat warming himself before the fire with his back towards the door. The sound of so many persons entering and leaving, and the scraping of the trunk as it was deposited upon the bare boards, were alike unable to attract the notice of the occupant; and Silas stood waiting, in an agony of fear, until he should deign to recognize his presence.

Perhaps five minutes had elapsed before the man turned leisurely about, and disclosed the features of Prince Florizel of Bohemia.

'So, sir,' he said, with great severity, 'this is the manner in which you abuse my politeness. You join yourselves to persons of condition, I perceive, for no other purpose than to escape the consequences of your crimes; and I can readily understand your embarrassment when I addressed myself to you yesterday.'

'Indeed,' cried Silas, 'I am innocent of everything except misfortune.'

And in a hurried voice, and with the greatest ingenuousness, he recounted to the prince the whole history of his calamity.

'I see I have been mistaken,' said his Highness, when he had heard him to an end. 'You are no other than a victim, and since I am not to punish, you may be sure I shall do my utmost to help. And now,' he continued, 'to business. Open your box at once, and let me see what it contains.'

Silas changed colour.

'I almost fear to look upon it,' he exclaimed.

'Nay,' replied the prince, 'have you not looked at it already? This is a form of sentimentality to be resisted. The sight of a sick man, whom we can still help, should appeal more directly to the feelings than that of a dead man who is equally beyond help or harm, love or hatred. Nerve yourself, Mr Scuddamore,' and then, seeing that Silas still hesitated, 'I do not desire to give another name to my request,' he added.

The young American awoke as if out of a dream, and with a shiver of repugnance, addressed himself to loose the straps and open the lock of the Saratoga trunk. The prince stood by, watching with a composed countenance and his hands behind his back. The body was quite stiff, and it cost Silas a great effort, both moral and physical, to dislodge it from its position, and discover the face.

Prince Florizel started back with an exclamation of painful surprise.

'Alas!' he cried, 'you little know, Mr Scuddamore, what a cruel gift you have brought me. This is a young man of my own suite, the brother of my trusted friend; and it was upon matters of my own service that he has thus perished at the hands of violent and treacherous men. Poor Geraldine,' he went on, as if to himself, 'in what words am I to tell you of your brother's fate? How can I excuse myself in your eyes, or in the eyes of God, for the presumptuous schemes that led him to this bloody and unnatural death? Ah, Florizel! Florizel! When will you learn the discretion that suits mortal life, and be no longer dazzled with the image of power at your disposal? Power!' he cried; 'who is more powerless? I look upon this young man whom I have sacrificed, Mr Scuddamore, and feel how small a thing it is to be a prince.'

Silas was moved at the sight of his emotion. He tried to murmur some consolatory words, and burst into tears.

The prince, touched by his obvious intention, came up to him and took him by the hand.

'Command yourself,' said he. 'We have both much to learn, and we shall both be better men for today's meeting.'

Silas thanked him in silence with an affectionate look.

'Write me the address of Doctor Noel on this piece of paper,' continued the prince, leading him towards the table; 'and let me recommend you, when you are again in Paris, to avoid the society of that dangerous man. He has acted in this matter on a generous inspiration; that I must believe; had he been privy to young Geraldine's death he would never have despatched the body to the care of the actual criminal.'

'The actual criminal!' repeated Silas in astonishment.

'Even so,' returned the prince. 'This letter, which the disposition of Almighty Providence has so strangely delivered into my hands, was addressed to no less a person than the criminal himself, the infamous president of the Suicide Club. Seek to pry no further in these perilous affairs, but content yourself with your own miraculous escape, and leave this house at once. I have pressing affairs, and must arrange at once about this poor clay, which was so lately a gallant and handsome youth.'

Silas took a grateful and submissive leave of Prince Florizel, but he lingered in Box Court until he saw him depart in a splendid carriage on a visit to Colonel Henderson of the police. Republican as he was, the young American took off his hat with almost a sentiment of devotion to the retreating carriage. And the same night, he started by rail on his return to Paris.

Here (observes my Arabian author) is the end of the STORY OF THE PHYSICIAN AND THE SARATOGA TRUNK. Omitting some reflections on the power of Providence, highly pertinent in the original, but little suited to our Occiddental taste, I shall only add that Mr Scuddamore has already begun to mount the ladder of political fame, and by last advices was the Sheriff of his native town.

3

THE ADVENTURE OF THE HANSOM CAB

Lieutenant Brackenbury Rich had greatly distinguished himself in one of the lesser Indian hill wars. He it was who took the chieftain prisoner with his own hand; his gallantry was universally applauded; and when he came home, prostrated by an ugly sabre cut and a protracted jungle fever, society was prepared to welcome the lieutenant as a celebrity of minor lustre. But his was a character remarkable for unaffected modesty; adventure was dear to his heart, but he cared little for adulation; and he waited at foreign watering places and in Algiers until the fame of his exploits had run through its nine days' vitality and begun to be forgotten. He arrived in London at last, in the early season, with as little observation as he could desire; and as he was an orphan and had none but distant relatives who lived in the provinces, it was almost as a foreigner that he installed himself in the capital of the country for which he had shed his blood.

On the day following his arrival he dined alone at a military club. He shook hands with a few old comrades, and received their warm congratulations; but as one and all had some engagement for the evening, he found himself left entirely to his own resources. He was in dress, for he had entertained the notion of visiting a theatre. But the great city was new to him; he had gone from a provincial school to a military college, and thence direct to the Eastern Empire; and he promised himself a variety of delights in this world for exploration. Swinging his cane, he took his way westward. It was a mild evening, already dark, and now and then threatening rain. The succession of faces in the lamplight stirred the Lieutenant's imagination; and it seemed to him as if he could walk for ever in that stimulating city atmosphere and surrounded by the mystery of four million private lives. He glanced at the houses, and marvelled what was passing behind those warmly-lighted windows; he looked into face after face, and saw them each intent upon some unknown interest, criminal or kindly.

'They talk of war,' he thought, 'but this is the great battlefield of mankind.'

And then he began to wonder that he should walk so long in this complicated scene, and not chance upon so much as the shadow of an adventure for himself.

'All in good time,' he reflected. 'I am still a stranger, and perhaps wear a strange air. But I must be drawn into the eddy before long.'

The night was already well advanced when a plump of cold rain fell suddenly out of the darkness. Brackenbury paused under some trees, and as he did so he caught sight of a hansom cabman making him a sign that he was disengaged. The circumstance fell in so happily to the occasion, that he at once raised his cane in answer, and had soon ensconced himself in the London gondola.

'Where to, sir?' asked the driver.

'Where you please,' said Brackenbury.

And immediately, at a pace of surprising swiftness, the hansom drove off through the rain into a maze of villas. One villa was so like another, each with its front garden, and there was so little to distinguish the deserted lamp-lit streets and crescents through which the flying hansom took its way, that Brackenbury soon lost all idea of direction.

He would have been tempted to believe that the cabman was amusing himself by driving him round and round and in and out about a small quarter, but there was something businesslike in the speed which convinced him of the contrary. The man had an object in view, he was hastening towards a definite end; and Brackenbury was at once astonished at the fellow's skill in picking a way through such a labyrinth, and a little concerned to imagine what was the occasion of his hurry. He had heard tales of strangers falling ill in London. Did the driver belong to some bloody and treacherous association? And was he himself being whirled to a murderous death?

The thought had scarcely presented itself, when the cab swung sharply round a corner and pulled up before the garden gate of a villa in a long and wide road. The house was brilliantly lighted up. Another hansom had just driven away, and Brackenbury could see a gentleman being admitted at the front door and received by several liveried servants. He was surprised that the cabman should have stopped so immediately in front of a house where a reception was being held; but he did not doubt it was the result of accident, and sat placidly smoking where he was, until he heard the trap thrown open over his head.

'Here we are, sir,' said the driver.

'Here!' repeated Brackenbury. 'Where?'

'You told me to take you where I pleased, sir,' returned the man with a chuckle, 'and here we are.'

It struck Brackenbury that the voice was wonderfully smooth and courteous for a man in so inferior a position; he remembered the speed at which he had been driven; and now it occurred to him that the hansom was more luxuriously appointed than the common run of public conveyances.

'I must ask you to explain,' said he. 'Do you mean to turn me out into the rain? My good man, I suspect the choice is mine.'

'The choice is certainly yours,' replied the driver; 'but when I tell you all, I believe I know how a gentleman of your figure will decide. There is a gentlemen's party in this house. I do not know whether the master be a stranger to London and without acquaintances of his own; or whether he is a man of odd notions. But certainly I was hired to kidnap single gentlemen in evening dress, as many as I pleased, but military officers by preference. You have simply to go in and say that Mr Morris invited you.'

'Are you Mr Morris?' inquired the lieutenant.

'Oh, no,' replied the cabman. 'Mr Morris is the person of the house.'

'It is not a common way of collecting guests,' said Brackenbury: 'but an eccentric man might very well indulge the whim without any intention to offend. And suppose that I refuse Mr Morris's invitation,' he went on, 'what then?'

'My orders are to drive you back where I took you from,' replied the man, 'and set out to look for others up to midnight. Those who have no fancy for such an adventure, Mr Morris said, were not the guests for him.'

These words decided the lieutenant on the spot.

'After all,' he reflected, as he descended from the hansom, 'I have not had long to wait for my adventure.'

He had hardly found footing on the sidewalk, and was still feeling in his pocket for the fare, when the cab swung about and drove off by the way it came at the former breakneck velocity. Brackenbury shouted after the man, who paid no heed, and continued to drive away; but the sound of his voice was overheard in the house, the door was again thrown open, emitting a flood of light upon the garden, and a servant ran down to meet him holding an umbrella.

'The cabman has been paid,' observed the servant in a very civil tone; and he proceeded to escort Brackenbury along the path and up the steps. In the hall, several other attendants relieved him of his hat, cane, and paletot, gave him a ticket with a number in return, and politely hurried him up a stair adorned with tropical flowers, to the door of an apartment on the first storey. Here, a grave butler inquired his name, and announcing 'Lieutenant Brackenbury Rich', ushered him into the drawing room of the house.

A young man, slender and singularly handsome, came forward and greeted him with an air at once courtly and affectionate. Hundreds of candles, of the finest wax, lit up a room that was perfumed, like the staircase, with a profusion of rare and beautiful flowering shrubs. A side-table was loaded with tempting viands. Several servants went to and fro with fruits and goblets of champagne. The company was perhaps sixteen in number, all men, few beyond the prime of life, and with hardly an exception, of a dashing and capable exterior. They were divided into two groups, one about a roulette board, and the other surrounding a table at which one of their number held a bank of baccarat.

'I see,' thought Brackenbury, 'I am in a private gambling saloon, and the cabman was a tout.'

His eye had embraced the details, and his mind formed the conclusion, while his host was still holding him by the hand; and to him his looks returned from this rapid survey. At a second view Mr Morris surprised him still more than on the first. The easy elegance of his manners, the distinction, amiability, and courage that appeared upon his features, fitted very ill with the lieutenant's preconceptions on the subject of the proprietor of a hell; and the tone of his conversation seemed to mark him out for a man of position and merit. Brackenbury found he had an instinctive liking for his entertainer; and though he chid himself for the weakness, he was unable to resist a sort of friendly attraction for Mr Morris's person and character.

'I have heard of you, Lieutenant Rich,' said Mr Morris, lowering his tone; 'and believe me I am gratified to make your acquaintance. Your looks accord with the reputation that has preceded you from India. And if you will forget for a while the irregularity of your presentation in my house, I shall feel it not only an honour, but a genuine pleasure besides. A man who makes a mouthful of barbarian cavaliers,' he added with a laugh, 'should not be appalled by a breach of etiquette, however serious.'

And he led him towards the sideboard and pressed him to partake of some refreshment.

'Upon my word,' the lieutenant reflected, 'this is one of the pleasantest fellows and, I do not doubt, one of the most agreeable societies in London.'

He partook of some champagne, which he found excellent; and observing that many of the company were already smoking, he lit one of his own Manillas, and strolled up to the roulette board, where he sometimes made a stake and sometimes looked on smilingly on the fortune of others. It was while he was thus idling that he became aware of a sharp scrutiny to which the whole of the guests were subjected. Mr Morris went here and there, ostensibly busied on hospitable concerns; but he had ever a shrewd glance at disposal; not a man of the party escaped his sudden, searching looks; he took stock of the bearing of heavy losers, he valued the amount of the stakes, he paused behind couples who were deep in conversation; and, in a word, there was hardly a characteristic of any one present but he seemed to catch and make a note of it. Brackenbury began to wonder if this were indeed a gambling hell: it had so much the air of a private inquisition. He followed Mr Morris in all his movements; and although the man had a ready smile, he seemed to perceive, as it were under a mask, a haggard, careworn, and preoccupied spirit. The fellows around him laughed and made their game; but Brackenbury had lost interest in the guests.

'This Morris,' thought he, 'is no idler in the room. Some deep purpose inspires him; let it be mine to fathom it.'

Now and then Mr Morris would call one of his visitors aside; and after a brief colloquy in an anteroom, he would return alone, and the visitors in question reappeared no more. After a certain number of repetitions, this performance excited Brackenbury's curiosity to a high degree. He determined to be at the bottom of this minor mystery at once; and strolling into the anteroom, found a deep window recess concealed by curtains of the fashionable green. Here he hurriedly ensconced himself; nor had he to wait long, before the sound of steps and voices drew near him from the principal apartment. Peering through the division, he saw Mr Morris escorting a fat and ruddy personage, with somewhat the look of a commercial traveller, whom Brackenbury had already remarked for his coarse laugh and under-bred behaviour at the table. The pair halted immediately before the window, so that Brackenbury lost not a word of the following discourse:—

'I beg you a thousand pardons!' began Mr Morris, with the most conciliatory manner; 'and, if I appear rude, I am sure you will readily forgive me. In a place so great as London, accidents must continually happen; and the best that we can hope is to remedy them with as small delay as possible. I will not deny that I fear you have made a mistake and honoured my poor house by inadvertence; for, to speak openly, I cannot at all remember your appearance. Let me put the question without unnecessary circumlocution—between gentlemen of honour a word will suffice— Under whose roof do you suppose yourself to be?'

'That of Mr Morris,' replied the other, with a prodigious display of confusion, which had been visibly growing upon him throughout the last few words.

'Mr John or Mr James Morris?' inquired the host.

'I really cannot tell you,' returned the unfortunate guest. 'I am not personally acquainted with the gentleman, any more than I am with yourself.'

'I see,' said Mr Morris. 'There is another person of the same name farther down the street; and I have no doubt the policeman will be able to supply you with his number. Believe me, I felicitate myself on the misunderstanding which has procured me the pleasure of your company for so long; and let me express a hope that we may meet again upon a more regular footing. Meantime, I would not for the world detain you longer from your friends. John,' he added, raising his voice, 'will you see that this gentleman finds his greatcoat?'

And with the most agreeable air, Mr Morris escorted his visitor as far as the anteroom door, where he left him under conduct of the butler. As he passed the window, on his return to the drawing room, Brackenbury could hear him utter a profound sigh, as though his mind was loaded with a great anxiety, and his nerves already fatigued with the task on which he was engaged.

For perhaps an hour, the hansoms kept arriving with such frequency, that Mr Morris had to receive a new guest for every old one that he sent away, and the company preserved its number undiminished. But towards the end of that time the arrivals grew few and far between, and at length ceased entirely, while the process of elimination was continued with unimpaired activity. The drawing room began to look empty: the baccarat was discontinued for lack of a banker; more than one person said good-night of his own accord, and was suffered to depart without expostulation; and in the meanwhile Mr Morris redoubled in agreeable attentions to those who stayed behind. He went from group to group and from person to person with looks of the readiest sympathy and the most pertinent and pleasing talk; he was not so much like a host as like a hostess, and there was a feminine coquetry and condescension in his manner which charmed the hearts of all.

As the guests grew thinner, Lieutenant Rich strolled for a moment out of the drawing room into the hall in quest of fresher air. But he had no sooner passed the threshold of the antechamber than he was brought to a dead halt by a discovery of the most surprising nature. The flowering shrubs had disappeared from the staircase; three large furniture wagons stood before the garden gate; the servants were busy dismantling the house upon all sides; and some of them had already donned their greatcoats and were preparing to depart. It was like the end of a country ball, where everything has been supplied by contract. Brackenbury had indeed some matter for reflection. First, the guests, who were no real guests after all, had been dismissed; and now the servants, who could hardly be genuine servants, were actively dispersing.

"Was the whole establishment a sham?' he asked himself. 'The mushroom of a single night which should disappear before morning?'

Watching a favourable opportunity, Brackenbury dashed upstairs to the highest regions of the house. It was as he had expected. He ran from room to room, and saw not a stick of furniture nor so much as a picture on the walls. Although the house had been painted and papered, it was not only uninhabited at present, but plainly had never been inhabited at all. The young officer remembered with astonishment its specious, settled, and hospitable air on his arrival. It was only at a prodigious cost that the imposture could have been carried out upon so great a scale.

Who, then, was Mr Morris? What was his intention in thus playing the householder for a single night in the remote west of London? And why did he collect his visitors at hazard from the streets?

Brackenbury remembered that he had already delayed too long, and hastened to join the company. Many had left during his absence; and counting the lieutenant and his host, there were not more than five persons in the drawing room—recently so thronged. Mr Morris greeted him, as he re-entered the apartment, with a smile, and immediately rose to his feet.

'It is now time, gentlemen,' said he, 'to explain my purpose in decoying you from your amusements. I trust you did not find the evening hang very dully on your hands; but my object, I will confess it, was not to entertain your leisure, but to help myself in an unfortunate necessity. You are all gentlemen,' he continued, 'your appearance does you that much justice, and I ask for no better security. Hence, I speak it without concealment, I ask you to render me a dangerous and delicate service; dangerous because you may run the hazard of your lives, and delicate because I must ask an absolute discretion upon all that you shall see or hear. From an utter stranger the request is almost comically extravagant; I am well aware of this; and I would add at once, if there be any one present who has heard enough, if there be one among the party who recoils from a dangerous confidence and a piece of Quixotic devotion to he knows not whom—here is my hand ready, and I shall wish him good-night and Godspeed with all the sincerity in the world.'

A very tall, black man, with a heavy stoop, immediately responded to this appeal.

'I commend your frankness, sir,' said he; 'and, for my part, I go. I make no reflections; but I cannot deny that you fill me with suspicious thoughts. I go myself, as I say; and perhaps you will think I have no right to add words to my example.'

'On the contrary,' replied Mr Morris, 'I am obliged to you for all you say. It would be impossible to exaggerate the gravity of my proposal.'

'Well, gentlemen, what do you say?' said the tall man, addressing the others. 'We have had our evening's frolic; shall we all go homeward peaceably in a body? You will think well of my suggestion in the morning, when you see the sun again in innocence and safety.'

The speaker pronounced the last words with an intonation which added to their force; and his face wore a singular expression, full of gravity and significance. Another of the company rose hastily, and, with some appearance of alarm, prepared to take his leave. There were only two who held their ground, Brackenbury and an old red-nosed cavalry major; but these two preserved a nonchalant demeanour, and, beyond a look of intelligence which they rapidly exchanged, appeared entirely foreign to the discussion that had just been terminated.

Mr Morris conducted the deserters as far as the door, which he closed upon their heels; then he turned round, disclosing a countenance of mingled relief and animation, and addressed the two officers as follows.

'I have chosen my men like Joshua in the Bible,' said Mr Morris, 'and I now believe I have the pick of London. Your appearance pleased my hansom cabmen; then it delighted me; I have watched your behaviour in a strange company, and under the most unusual circumstances: I have studied how you played and how you bore your losses; lastly, I have put you to the test of a staggering announcement, and you received it like an invitation to dinner. It is not for nothing,' he cried, 'that I have been for years the companion and the pupil of the bravest and wisest potentate in Europe.'

'At the affair of Bunderchang,' observed the major, 'I asked for twelve volunteers, and every trooper in the ranks replied to my appeal. But a gaming party is not the same thing as a regiment under fire. You may be pleased, I suppose, to have found two, and two who will not fail you at a push. As for the pair who ran away, I count them among the most pitiful hounds I ever met with. Lieutenant Rich,' he added, addressing Brackenbury, 'I have heard much of you of late; and I cannot doubt but you have also heard of me. I am Major O'Rooke.'

And the veteran tendered his hand, which was red and tremulous, to the young lieutenant.

'Who has not?' answered Brackenbury.

'When this little matter is settled,' said Mr Morris, 'you will think I have sufficiently rewarded you; for I could offer neither a more valuable service than to make him acquainted with the other.'

'And now,' said Major O'Rooke, 'is it a duel?'

'A duel after a fashion,' replied Mr Morris, 'a duel with unknown and dangerous enemies, and, as I gravely fear, a duel to the death. I must ask you,' he continued, 'to call me Morris no longer; call me, if you please, Hammersmith; my real name, as well as that of another person to whom I hope to present you before long, you will gratify me by not asking and not seeking to discover for yourselves. Three days ago the person of whom I speak disappeared suddenly from home; and, until this morning, I received no hint of his situation. You will fancy my alarm when I tell you that he is engaged upon a work of private justice. Bound by an unhappy oath, too lightly sworn, he finds it necessary, without the help of law, to rid the earth of an insidious and bloody villain. Already two of our friends, and one of them my own born brother, have perished in the enterprise. He himself, or I am much deceived, is taken in the same fatal toils. But at least he still lives and still hopes, as this billet sufficiently proves.'

And the speaker, no other than Colonel Geraldine, proffered a letter, thus conceived:

'Major Hammersmith,—On Wednesday, at 3 A.M., you will be admitted by the small door to the gardens of Rochester House, Regent's Park, by a man who is entirely in my interest. I must request you not to fail me by a second. Pray bring my case of swords, and, if you can find them, one or two gentlemen of conduct and discretion to whom my person is unknown. My name must not be used in this affair.
'T. GODALL.'

'From his wisdom alone, if he had no other title,' pursued Colonel Geraldine, when the others had each satisfied his curiosity, 'my friend is a man whose directions should implicitly be followed. I need not tell you, therefore, that I have not so much as visited the neighbourhood of Rochester House; and that I am still as wholly in the dark as either of yourselves as to the nature of my friend's dilemma. I betook myself, as soon as I had received this order, to a furnishing contractor, and, in a few hours, the house in which we now are had assumed its late air of festival. My scheme was at least original; and I am far from regretting an action which has procured me the services of Major O'Rooke and Lieutenant Brackenbury Rich. But the servants in the street will have a strange awakening. The house which this evening was full of lights and visitors they will find uninhabited and for sale tomorrow morning. Thus even the most serious concerns,' added the colonel, 'have a merry side.'

'And let us add a merry ending,' said Brackenbury.

The colonel consulted his watch.

'It is now hard on two,' he said. 'We have an hour before us, and a swift cab is at the door. Tell me if I may count upon your help.'

'During a long life,' replied Major O'Rooke, 'I never took back my hand from anything, nor so much as hedged a bet.'

Brackenbury signified his readiness in the most becoming terms; and after they had drunk a glass or two of wine, the colonel gave each of them a loaded revolver, and the three mounted into the cab and drove off for the address in question.

Rochester House was a magnificent residence on the banks of the canal. The large extent of the garden isolated it in an unusual degree from the annoyances of neighbourhood. It seemed the parc aux cerfs of some great nobleman or millionaire. As far as could be seen from the street, there was not a glimmer of light in any of the numerous windows of the mansion; and the place had a look of neglect, as though the master had been long from home.

The cab was discharged, and the three gentlemen were not long in discovering the small door, which was a sort of postern in a lane between two garden walls. It still wanted ten or fifteen minutes of the appointed time; the rain fell heavily, and the adventurers sheltered themselves below some pendant ivy, and spoke in low tones of the approaching trial.

Suddenly, Geraldine raised his finger to command silence, and all three bent their hearing to the utmost. Through the continuous noise of the rain, the steps and voices of two men became audible from the other side of the wall; and, as they drew nearer, Brackenbury, whose sense of hearing was remarkably acute, could even distinguish some fragments of their talk.

'Is the grave dug?' asked one.

'It is,' replied the other; 'behind the laurel hedge. When the job is done, we can cover it with a pile of stakes.'

The first speaker laughed, and the sound of his merriment was shocking to the listeners on the other side.

'In an hour from now,' he said.

And by the sound of the steps it was obvious that the pair had separated, and were proceeding in contrary directions.

Almost immediately after the postern door was cautiously opened, a white face was protruded into the lane, and a hand was seen beckoning to the watchers. In dead silence, the three passed the door, which was immediately locked behind them, and followed their guide through several garden alleys to the kitchen entrance of the house. A single candle burned in the great paved kitchen, which was destitute of the customary furniture; and as the party proceeded to ascend from thence by a flight of winding stairs, a prodigious noise of rats testified still more plainly to the dilapidation of the house.

Their conductor preceded them, carrying the candle. He was a lean man, much bent, but still agile; and he turned from time to time and admonished silence and caution by his gestures. Colonel Geraldine followed on his heels, the case of swords under one arm, and a pistol ready in the other. Brackenbury's heart beat thickly. He perceived that they were still in time; but he judged from the alacrity of the old man that the hour of action must be near at hand; and the circumstances of this adventure were so obscure and menacing, the place seemed so well chosen for the darkest acts, that an older man than Brackenbury might have been pardoned a measure of emotion as he closed the procession up the winding stair.

At the top, the guide threw open a door and ushered the three officers before him into a small apartment, lighted by a smoky lamp and the glow of a modest fire. At the chimney corner sat a man in the early prime of life, and of a stout but courtly and commanding appearance. His attitude and expression were those of the most unmoved composure; he was smoking a cheroot with much enjoyment and deliberation, and on a table by his elbow stood a long glass of some effervescing beverage which diffused an agreeable odour through the room.

'Welcome,' said he, extending his hand to colonel Geraldine. 'I knew I might count on your exactitude.'

'On my devotion,' replied the colonel, with a bow.

'Present me to your friends,' continued the first; and, when that ceremony had been performed, 'I wish, gentlemen,' he added, with the most exquisite affability, 'that I could offer you a more cheerful programme; it is ungracious to inaugurate an acquaintance upon serious affairs; but the compulsion of events is stronger than the obligations of good-fellowship. I hope and believe you will be able to forgive me this unpleasant evening; and for men of your stamp it will be enough to know that you are conferring a considerable favour.'

'Your Highness,' said the major, 'must pardon my bluntness. I am unable to hide what I know. For some time back I have suspected Major Hammersmith, but Mr Godall is unmistakable. To seek two men in London unacquainted with Prince Florizel of Bohemia was to ask too much at Fortune's hands.'

'Prince Florizel!' cried Brackenbury in amazement.

And he gazed with the deepest interest on the features of the celebrated personage before him.

'I shall not lament the loss of my incognito,' remarked the prince, 'for it enables me to thank you with the more authority. You would have done as much for Mr Godall, I feel sure, as for the Prince of Bohemia; but the latter can perhaps do more for you. The gain is mine,' he added, with a courteous gesture.

And the next moment he was conversing with the two officers about the Indian army and the native troops, a subject on which, as on all others, he had a remarkable fund of information and the soundest views.

There was something so striking in this man's attitude at a moment of deadly peril that Brackenbury was overcome with respectful admiration; nor was he less sensible to the charm of his conversation or the surprising amenity of his address. Every gesture, every intonation, was not only noble in itself, but seemed to ennoble the fortunate mortal for whom it was intended; and Brackenbury confessed to himself with enthusiasm that this was a sovereign for whom a brave man might thankfully lay down his life.

Many minutes had thus passed, when the person who had introduced them into the house, and who had sat ever since in a corner, and with his watch in his hand, arose and whispered a word into the prince's ear.

'It is well, Dr Noel,' replied Florizel, aloud; and then addressing the others, 'You will excuse me, gentlemen,' he added, 'if I have to leave you in the dark. The moment now approaches.'

Dr Noel extinguished the lamp. A faint, grey light, premonitory of the dawn, illuminated the window, but was not sufficient to illuminate the room; and when the prince rose to his feet, it was impossible to distinguish his features or to make a guess at the nature of the emotion which obviously affected him as he spoke. He moved towards the door, and placed himself at one side of it in an attitude of the wariest attention.

'You will have the kindness,' he said, 'to maintain the strictest silence, and to conceal yourselves in the densest of the shadow.'

The three officers and the physician hastened to obey, and for nearly ten minutes the only sound in Rochester House was occasioned by the excursions of the rats behind the woodwork. At the end of that period, a loud creak of a hinge broke in with surprising distinctness on the silence; and shortly after, the watchers could distinguish a slow and cautious tread approaching up the kitchen stair. At every second step the intruder seemed to pause and lend an ear, and during these intervals, which seemed of an incalculable duration, a profound disquiet possessed the spirit of the listeners. Dr Noel, accustomed as he was to dangerous emotions, suffered an almost pitiful physical prostration; his breath whistled in his lungs, his teeth grated one upon another, and his joints cracked aloud as he nervously shifted his position.

At last, a hand was laid upon the door, and the bolt shot back with a slight report. There followed another pause, during which Brackenbury could see the prince draw himself together noiselessly as if for some unusual exertion. Then the door opened, letting in a little more of the light of the morning; and the figure of a man appeared upon the threshold and stood motionless. He was tall, and carried a knife in his hand. Even in the twilight they could see his upper teeth bare and glistening, for his mouth was open like that of a hound about to leap. The man had evidently been over the head in water but a minute or two before; and even while he stood there the drops kept falling from his wet clothes and pattered on the floor.

The next moment he crossed the threshold. There was a leap, a stifled cry, an instantaneous struggle; and before Colonel Geraldine could spring to his aid, the prince held the man disarmed and helpless, by the shoulders

'Dr Noel,' he said, 'you will be so good as to re-light the lamp.'

And relinquishing the charge of his prisoner to Geraldine and Brackenbury, he crossed the room and set his back against the chimney-piece. As soon as the lamp had kindled, the party beheld an unaccustomed sternness on the prince's features. It was no longer Florizel, the careless gentleman; it was the Prince of Bohemia, justly incensed and full of deadly purpose, who now raised his head and addressed the captive president of the Suicide Club.

'President,' he said, 'you have laid your last snare, and your own feet are taken in it. The day is beginning; it is your last morning. You have just swum the Regent's Canal; it is your last bathe in this world. Your old accomplice, Dr Noel, so far from betraying me, has delivered you into my hands for judgment. And the grave you had dug for me this afternoon shall serve, in God's almighty providence, to hide your own just doom from the curiosity of mankind. Kneel and pray, sir, if you have a mind that way; for your time is short, and God is weary of your iniquities.'

The president made no answer either by word or sign; but continued to hang his head and gaze sullenly on the floor, as though he were conscious of the prince's prolonged and unsparing regard.

'Gentlemen,' continued Florizel, resuming the ordinary tone of his conversation, 'this is a fellow who has long eluded me, but whom, thanks to Dr Noel, I now have tightly by the heels. To tell the story of his misdeeds would occupy more time than we can now afford; but if the canal had contained nothing but the blood of his victims, I believe the wretch would have been no drier than you see him. Even in an affair of this sort I desire to preserve the forms of honour. But I make you the judges, gentlemen—this is more an execution than a duel and to give the rogue his choice of weapons would be to push too far a point of etiquette. I cannot afford to lose my life in such a business,' he continued, unlocking the case of swords; 'and as a pistol-bullet travels so often on the wings of chance, and skill and courage may fall by the most trembling marksman, I have decided, and I feel sure you will approve my determination, to put this question to the touch of swords.'

When Brackenbury and Major O'Rooke, to whom these remarks were particularly addressed, had each intimated his approval, 'Quick, sir,' added Prince Florizel to the president, 'choose a blade and do not keep me waiting; I have an impatience to be done with you for ever.'

For the first time since he was captured and disarmed, the president raised his head, and it was plain that he began instantly to pluck up courage.

'Is it to be stand up?' he asked eagerly, 'and between you and me?'

'I mean so far to honour you,' replied the prince.

'Oh, come!' cried the president. 'With a fair field, who knows how things may happen? I must add that I consider it handsome behaviour on your Highness's part; and if the worst comes to the worst, I shall die by one of the most gallant gentlemen in Europe.'

And the president, liberated by those who had detained him, stepped up to the table and began, with minute attention, to select a sword. He was highly elated, and seemed to feel no doubt that he should issue victorious from the contest. The spectators grew alarmed in the face of so entire a confidence, and adjured Prince Florizel to reconsider his intention.

'It is but a farce,' he answered; 'and I think I can promise you, gentlemen, that it will not be long a-playing.'

'Your Highness will be careful not to overreach,' said Colonel Geraldine.

'Geraldine,' returned the prince, 'did you ever know me fail in a debt of honour? I owe you this man's death, and you shall have it.'

The president at last satisfied himself with one of the rapiers, and signified his readiness by a gesture that was not devoid of a rude nobility. The nearness of peril, and the sense of courage, even to this obnoxious villain, lent an air of manhood and a certain grace.

The prince helped himself at random to a sword.

'Colonel Geraldine and Doctor Noel,' he said, 'will have the goodness to await me in this room. I wish no personal friend of mine to be involved in this transaction. Major O'Rooke, you are a man of some years and a settled reputation—let me recommend the president to your good graces. Lieutenant Rich will be so good as lend me his attentions: a young man cannot have too much experience in such affairs.'

'Your Highness,' replied Brackenbury, 'it is an honour I shall prize extremely.'

'It is well,' returned Prince Florizel; 'I shall hope to stand your friend in more important circumstances.'

And so saying, he led the way out of the apartment and down the kitchen stairs.

The two men who were thus left alone threw open the window and leaned out, straining every sense to catch an indication of the tragical events that were about to follow. The rain was now over; day had almost come, and the birds were piping in the shrubbery and on the forest trees of the garden. The prince and his companions were visible for a moment as they followed an alley between two flowering thickets; but at the first corner a clump of foliage intervened, and they were again concealed from view. This was all that the colonel and the physician had an opportunity to see, and the garden was so vast, and the place of combat evidently so remote from the house, that not even the noise of swordplay reached their ears.

'He has taken him towards the grave,' said Dr Noel, with a shudder.

'God,' cried the colonel, 'God defend the right!'

And they awaited the event in silence, the doctor shaking with fear, the colonel in an agony of sweat. Many minutes must have elapsed, the day was sensibly broader, and the birds were singing more heartily in the garden before a sound of returning footsteps recalled their glances towards the door. It was the prince and the two Indian officers who entered. God had defended the right.

'I am ashamed of my emotion,' said Prince Florizel; 'I feel

it is a weakness unworthy of my station, but the continued existence of that hound of hell had begun to prey upon me like a disease, and his death has more refreshed me than a night of slumber. Look, Geraldine,' he continued, throwing his sword upon the floor, 'there is the blood of the man who killed your brother. It should be a welcome sight. And yet,' he added, 'see how strangely we men are made! My revenge is not yet five minutes old, and already I am beginning to ask myself if even revenge be attainable on this precarious stage of life. The ill he did, who can undo it? The career in which he amassed a huge fortune (for the house itself in which we stand belonged to him)—that career is now a part of the destiny of mankind for ever; and I might weary myself making thrusts in carte until the crack of judgment, and Geraldine's brother would be none the less dead, and a thousand other innocent persons would be none the less dishonoured and debauched! The existence of a man is so small a thing to take, so mighty a thing to employ! Alas!' he cried, 'is there anything in life so disenchanting as attainment?'

'God's justice has been done,' replied the doctor. 'So much I behold. The lesson, your Highness, has been a cruel one for me; and I await my own turn with deadly apprehension.'

'What was I saying?' cried the prince. 'I have punished, and here is the man beside us who can help me to undo. Ah, Dr Noel! you and I have before us many a day of hard and honourable toil; and perhaps, before we have none, you may have more than redeemed your early errors.'

'And in the meantime,' said the doctor, 'let me go and bury my oldest friend.'

And this (observes the erudite Arabian) is the fortunate conclusion of the tale. The prince, it is superfluous to mention, forgot none of those who served him in this great exploit; and to this day his authority and influence help them forward in their public carreer, while his condescending friendship adds a charm to their private life. To collect, continues my author, all the strange events in which this prince has played the part of Providence, were to fill the habitable globe with books. But the stories which relate to the fortunes of THE RAJAH'S DIAMOND are of too entertaining a description, says he, to be omitted. Following prudently in the footsteps of this Oriental, we shall now begin the series to which he refers with the STORY OF THE BANDBOX.

4

STORY OF THE BANDBOX

Up to the age of sixteen, at a private school and afterwards at one of those great institutions for which England is justly famous, Mr Harry Hartley had received the ordinary education of a gentleman. At that period, he manifested a remarkable distaste for study; and his only surviving parent being both weak and ignorant, he was permitted thenceforward to spend his time in the attainment of petty and purely elegant accomplishments. Two years later, he was left an orphan and almost a beggar. For all active and industrious pursuits, Harry was unfitted alike by nature and training. He could sing romantic ditties, and accompany himself with discretion on the piano; he was a graceful although a timid cavalier; he had a pronounced taste for chess; and nature had sent him into the world with one of the most engaging exteriors that can well be fancied. Blond and pink, with dove's eyes and a gentle smile, he had an air of agreeable tenderness and melancholy, and the most submissive and caressing manners. But when all is said, he was not the man to lead armaments of war, or direct the councils of a State.

A fortunate chance and some influence obtained for Harry, at the time of his bereavement, the position of private secretary to Major-General Sir Thomas Vandeleur. C.B. Sir Thomas was a man of sixty, loud-spoken, boisterous, and domineering. For some reason, some service the nature of which had been often whispered and repeatedly denied, the Rajah of Kashgar had presented this officer with the sixth known diamond of the world. The gift transformed General Vandeleur from a poor into a wealthy man, from an obscure and unpopular soldier into one of the lions of London society; the possessor of the Rajah's Diamond was welcome in the most exclusive circles; and he had found a lady, young, beautiful, and well-born, who was willing to call the diamond hers even at the price of marriage with Sir Thomas Vandeleur. It was commonly said at the time that, as like draws to like, one jewel had attracted another; certainly Lady Vandeleur was not only a gem of the finest water in her own person, but she showed herself to the world in a very costly setting; and she was considered by many respectable authorities, as one among the three or four best dressed women in England.

Harry's duty as secretary was not particularly onerous; but he had a dislike for all prolonged work; it gave him pain to ink his fingers; and the charms of Lady Vandeleur and her toilettes drew him often from the library to the boudoir. He had the prettiest ways among women, could talk fashions with enjoyment, and was never more happy than when criticizing a shade of ribbon, or running on an errand to the milliner's. In short, Sir Thomas's correspondence fell into pitiful arrears, and my Lady had another lady's maid.

At last, the general, who was one of the least patient of military commanders, arose from his place in a violent access of passion, and indicated to his secretary that he had no further need for his services, with one of those explanatory gestures which are most rarely employed between gentlemen. The door being unfortunately open, Mr Hartley fell downstairs head foremost.

He arose somewhat hurt and very deeply aggrieved. The life in the general's house precisely suited him; he moved, on a more or less doubtful footing, in very genteel company, he did little, he ate of the best, and he had a lukewarm satisfaction in the presence of Lady Vandeleur, which, in his own heart, he dubbed by a more emphatic name.

Immediately after he had been outraged by the military foot, he hurried to the boudoir and recounted his sorrows.

'You know very well, my dear Harry,' replied Lady Vandeleur, for she called him by name like a child or a domestic servant, 'that you never by any chance do what the general tells you. No more do I, you may say. But that is different. A woman can earn her pardon for a good year of disobedience by a single adroit submission; and, besides, no one is married to his private secretary. I shall be sorry to lose you; but since you cannot stay longer in a house where you have been insulted, I shall wish you good-bye, and I promise you to make the general smart for his behaviour.'

Harry's countenance fell; tears came into his eyes, and he gazed on Lady Vandeleur with a tender reproach.

'My Lady,' said he, 'what is an insult? I should think little indeed of any one who could not forgive them by the score. But to leave one's friends; to tear up the bonds of affection—'

He was unable to continue, for his emotion choked him, and he began to weep.

Lady Vandeleur looked at him with a curious expression. 'This little fool,' she thought, 'imagines himself to be in love with me. Why should he not become my servant instead of the general's? He is good-natured, obliging, and understands dress; and besides it will keep him out of mischief. He is positively too pretty to be unattached.' That night she talked over the general, who was already somewhat ashamed of his vivacity; and Harry was transferred to the feminine department, where his life was little short of heavenly. He was always dressed with uncommon nicety, wore delicate flowers in his buttonhole, and could entertain a visitor with tact and pleasantry. He took a pride in servility to a beautiful woman; received Lady Vandeleur's commands as so many marks of favour; and was pleased to exhibit himself before other men, who derided and despised him, in his character of male lady's-maid and man milliner. Nor could he think enough of his existence from a moral point of view. Wickedness seemed to him an essentially male attribute, and to pass one's days with a delicate woman, and principally occupied about trimmings, was to inhabit an enchanted isle among the storms of life.

One fine morning he came into the drawing room and began to arrange some music on the top of the piano. Lady Vandeleur, at the other end of the apartment, was speaking somewhat eagerly with her brother, Charlie Pendragon, an elderly young man, much broken with dissipation, and very lame of one foot. The private secretary, to whose entrance they paid no regard, could not avoid overhearing a part of their conversation.

'Today or never,' said the lady. 'Once and for all, it shall be done today.'

'Today, if it must be,' replied the brother, with a sigh. 'But it is a false step, a ruinous step, Clara; and we shall live to repent it dismally.'

Lady Vandeleur looked her brother steadily and somewhat strangely in the face.

'You forget,' she said; 'the man must die at last.'

'Upon my word, Clara,' said Pendragon, 'I believe you are the most heartless rascal in England.'

'You men,' she returned, 'are so coarsely built, that you can never appreciate a shade of meaning. You are yourselves rapacious, violent, immodest, careless of distinction; and yet the least thought for the future shocks you in a woman. I have no patience with such stuff. You would despise in a common banker the imbecility that you expect to find in us.'

'You are very likely right,' replied her brother; 'you were always cleverer than I. And, anyway, you know my motto: The family before all.'

'Yes, Charlie,' she returned, taking his hand in hers, 'I know your motto better than you know it yourself. "And Clara before the family!" Is not that the second part of it? Indeed, you are the best of brothers, and I love you dearly.'

Mr Pendragon got up, looking a little confused by these family endearments.

'I had better not be seen,' said he. 'I understand my part to a miracle, and I'll keep an eye on the Tame Cat.'

'Do,' she replied. 'He is an abject creature, and might ruin all.'

She kissed the tips of her fingers to him daintily; and the brother withdrew by the boudoir and the back stair.

'Harry,' said Lady Vandeleur, turning towards the secretary as soon as they were alone, 'I have a commission for you this morning. But you shall take a cab; I cannot have my secretary freckled.'

She spoke the last words with emphasis and a look of half-motherly pride that caused great contentment to poor Harry; and he professed himself charmed to find an opportunity of serving her.

'It is another of our great secrets,' she went on archly, 'and no one must know of it but my secretary and me. Sir Thomas would make the saddest disturbance; and if you only knew how weary I am of these scenes! Oh, Harry, Harry, can you explain to me what makes you men so violent and unjust? But, indeed, I know you cannot; you are the only man in the world who knows nothing of these shameful passions; you are so good, Harry, and so kind; you, at least, can be a woman's friend; and, do you know? I think you make the others more ugly by comparison.'

'It is you,' said Harry gallantly, 'who are so kind to me. You treat me like—'

'Like a mother,' interposed Lady Vandeleur; 'I try to be a mother to you. Or, at least,' she corrected herself with a smile, 'almost a mother. I am afraid I am too young to be your mother really. Let us say a friend—a dear friend.'

She paused long enough to let her words take effect in Harry's sentimental quarters, but not long enough to allow him a reply.

'But all this is beside our purpose,' she resumed. 'You will find a bandbox in the left-hand side of the oak wardrobe; it is underneath the pink slip that I wore on Wednesday with my Mechlin. You will take it immediately to this address,' and she gave him a paper, 'but do not, on any account, let it out of your hands until you have received a receipt written by myself. Do you understand? Answer, if you please—answer! This is extremely important, and I must ask you to pay some attention.'

Harry pacified her by repeating her instructions perfectly; and she was just going to tell him more when General Vandeleur flung into the apartment, scarlet with anger, and holding a long and elaborate milliner's bill in his hand.

'Will you look at this, madam?' cried he. 'Will you have the goodness to look at this document? I know well enough you married me for my money, and I hope I can make as great allowances as any other man in the service; but, as sure as God made me, I mean to put a period to this disreputable prodigality.'

'Mr Hartley,' said Lady Vandeleur, 'I think you understand what you have to do. May I ask you to see to it at once?'

'Stop,' said the general, addressing Harry, 'one word before you go.' And then, turning again to Lady Vandeleur, 'What is this precious fellow's errand?' he demanded. 'I trust him no further than I do yourself, let me tell you. If he had as much as the rudiments of honesty, he would scorn to stay in this house; and what he does for his wages is a mystery to all the world. What is his errand, madam? And why are you hurrying him away?'

'I supposed you had something to say to me in private,' replied the lady.

'You spoke about an errand,' insisted the general. 'Do not attempt to deceive me in my present state of temper. You certainly spoke about an errand.'

'If you insist on making your servants privy to our humiliating dissensions,' replied Lady Vandeleur, 'perhaps I had better ask Mr Hartley to sit down. No?' she continued; 'then you may go, Mr Hartley. I trust you may remember all that you have heard in this room; it may be useful to you.'

Harry at once made his escape from the drawing room; and as he ran upstairs he could hear the general's voice upraised in declamation, and the thin tones of Lady Vandeleur planting icy repartees at every opening. How cordially he admired the wife! How skilfully she could evade an awkward question! with what secure effrontery she repeated her instructions under the very guns of the enemy! And on the other hand, how he detested the husband!

There had been nothing unfamiliar in the morning's events, for he was continually in the habit of serving Lady Vandeleur on secret missions, principally connected with millinery. There was a skeleton in the house, as he well knew. The bottomless extravagance and the unknown liabilities of the wife had long since swallowed her own fortune, and threatened day by day to engulf that of the husband. Once or twice in every year, exposure and ruin seemed imminent, and Harry kept trotting round to all sorts of furnishers' shops, telling small fibs, and paying small advances on the gross amount, until another term was tided over, and the lady and her faithful secretary breathed again. For Harry, in a double capacity, was heart and soul upon that side of the war: not only did he adore Lady Vandeleur and fear and dislike her husband, but he naturally sympathized with the love of finery, and his own single extravagance was at the tailor's.

He found the bandbox where it had been described, arranged his toilette with care, and left the house. The sun shone brightly; the distance he had to travel was considerable, and he remembered with dismay that the general's sudden irruption had prevented Lady Vandeleur from giving him money for a cab. On this sultry day there was every chance that his complexion would suffer severely; and to walk through so much of London with a bandbox on his arm was a humiliation almost insupportable to a youth of his character. He paused, and took counsel with himself. The Vandeleurs lived in Eaton Place; his destination was near Notting Hill; plainly, he might cross the Park by keeping well in the open and avoiding populous alleys; and he thanked his stars when he reflected that it was still comparatively early in the day.

Anxious to be rid of his incubus, he walked somewhat faster than his ordinary, and he was already some way through Kensington Gardens when, in a solitary spot among trees, he found himself confronted by the general.

'I beg your pardon, Sir Thomas,' observed Harry, politely falling on one side; for the other stood directly in his path.

'Where are you going, sir?' asked the general.

'I am taking a little walk among the trees,' replied the lad.

The general struck the bandbox with his cane.

'With that thing?' he cried; 'you lie, sir, and you know you lie!'

'Indeed, Sir Thomas,' returned Harry, 'I am not accustomed to be questioned in so high a key.'

'You do not understand your position,' said the general. 'You are my servant, and a servant of whom I have conceived the most serious suspicions. How do I know but that your box is full of teaspoons?'

'It contains a silk hat belonging to a friend,' said Harry.

'Very well,' replied General Vandeleur. 'Then I want to see your friend's silk hat. I have,' he added grimly, 'a singular curiosity for hats; and I believe you know me to be somewhat positive.'

'I beg your pardon, Sir Thomas, I am exceedingly grieved,' Harry apologized; 'but indeed this is a private affair.'

The general caught him roughly by the shoulder with one hand, while he raised his cane in the most menacing manner with the other. Harry gave himself up for lost; but at the same moment heaven vouchsafed him an unexpected defender in the person of Charlie Pendragon, who now strode forward from behind the trees.

'Come, come, general, hold your hand,' said he, 'this is neither courteous nor manly.'

'Aha!' cried the general, wheeling round upon his new antagonist, 'Mr Pendragon! And do you suppose, Mr Pendragon, that because I have had the misfortune to marry your sister, I shall suffer myself to be dogged and thwarted by a discredited and bankrupt libertine like you? My acquaintance with Lady Vandeleur, sir, has taken away all my appetite for the other members of her family.'

'And do you fancy, General Vandeleur,' retorted Charlie, 'that because my sister has had the misfortune to marry you, she there and then forfeited her rights and privileges as a lady? I own, sir, that by that action she did as much as anybody could to derogate from her position; but to me she is still a Pendragon.

I make it my business to protect her from ungentlemanly outrage, and if you were ten times her husband I would not permit her liberty to be restrained, nor her private messengers to be violently arrested.'

'How is that, Mr Hartley?' interrogated the general. 'Mr Pendragon is of my opinion, it appears. He too suspects that Lady Vandeleur has something to do with your friend's silk hat.'

Charlie saw that he had committed an unpardonable blunder, which he hastened to repair.

'How, sir?' he cried; 'I suspect, do you say? I suspect nothing. Only where I find strength abused and a man brutalizing his inferiors, I take the liberty to interfere.'

As he said these words he made a sign to Harry, which the latter was too dull or too much troubled to understand.

'In what way am I to construe your attitude, sir?' demanded Vandeleur.

'Why, sir, as you please,' returned Pendragon.

The general once more raised his cane, and made a cut for Charlie's head; but the latter, lame foot and all, evaded the blow with his umbrella, ran in, and immediately closed with his formidable adversary.

'Run, Harry, run!' he cried; 'run, you dolt!'

Harry stood petrified for a moment, watching the two men sway together in this fierce embrace; then he turned and took to his heels. When he cast a glance over his shoulder he saw the general prostrate under Charlie's knee, but still making desperate efforts to reverse the situation; and the Gardens seemed to have filled with people, who were running from all directions towards the scene of fight. This spectacle lent the secretary wings; and he did not relax his pace until he had gained the Bayswater road, and plunged at random into an unfrequented by-street.

To see two gentlemen of his acquaintance thus brutally

mauling each other, was deeply shocking to Harry. He desired to forget the sight; he desired, above all, to put as great a distance as possible between himself and General Vandeleur; and in his eagerness for this he forgot everything about his destination, and hurried before him headlong and trembling. When he remembered that Lady Vandeleur was the wife of one and the sister of the other of these gladiators, his heart was touched with sympathy for a woman so distressingly misplaced in life. Even his own situation in the general's household looked hardly so pleasing as usual in the light of these violent transactions.

He had walked some little distance, busied with these meditations, before a slight collision with another passenger reminded him of the bandbox on his arm.

'Heavens!' cried he, 'where was my head? And whither have I wandered?'

Thereupon he consulted the envelope which Lady Vandeleur had given him. The address was there, but without a name. Harry was simply directed to ask for 'the gentleman who expected a parcel from Lady Vandeleur', and if he were not at home, to await his return. The gentleman, added the note, should present a receipt in the handwriting of the lady herself. All this seemed mightily mysterious, and Harry was above all astonished at the omission of the name and the formality of the receipt. He had thought little of this last when he heard it dropped in conversation; but reading it in cold blood, and taking it in connection with the other strange particulars, he became convinced that he was engaged in perilous affairs. For half a moment he had a doubt of Lady Vandeleur herself; for he found these obscure proceedings somewhat unworthy of so high a lady, and became more critical when her secrets were preserved against himself. But her empire over his spirit was too complete; he dismissed his suspicions, and blamed himself roundly for having so much as entertained them.

In one thing, however, his duty and interest, his generosity and his terrors, coincided—to get rid of the bandbox with the greatest possible despatch.

He accosted the first policeman and courteously inquired his way. It turned out that he was already not far from his destination, and a walk of a few minutes brought him to a small house in a lane, freshly painted, and kept with the most scrupulous attention. The knocker and bell-pull were highly polished; flowering pot-herbs garnished the sills of the different windows; and curtains of some rich material concealed the interior from the eyes of curious passengers. The place had an air of repose and secrecy; and Harry was so far caught with this spirit that he knocked with more than usual discretion, and was more than usually careful to remove all impurity from his boots.

A servant-maid of some personal attractions immediately opened the door, and seemed to regard the secretary with no unkind eyes.

'This is the parcel from Lady Vandeleur,' said Harry.

'I know,' replied the maid, with a nod. 'But the gentleman is from home. Will you leave it with me?'

'I cannot,' answered Harry. 'I am directed not to part with it but upon a certain condition, and I must ask you, I am afraid, to let me wait.'

'Well,' said she, 'I suppose I may let you wait. I am lonely enough, I can tell you, and you do not look as though you would eat a girl. But be sure and do not ask the gentleman's name, for that I am not to tell you.'

'Do you say so?' cried Harry. 'Why, how strange! But indeed for some time back I walk among surprises. One question I think I may surely ask without indiscretion: Is he the master of this house?'

'He is a lodger, and not eight days old at that,' returned

the maid. 'And now a question for a question: Do you know lady Vandeleur?'

'I am her private secretary,' replied Harry with a glow of modest pride.

'She is pretty, is she not?' pursued the servant.

'Oh, beautiful!' cried Harry; 'wonderfully lovely, and not less good and kind!'

'You look kind enough yourself,' she retorted; 'and I wager you are worth a dozen Lady Vandeleurs.'

Harry was properly scandalized.

'I!' he cried. 'I am only a secretary!'

'Do you mean that for me?' said the girl. 'Because I am only a housemaid, if you please.' And then, relenting at the sight of Harry's obvious confusion, 'I know you mean nothing of the sort,' she added; 'and I like your looks; but I think nothing of your Lady Vandeleur. Oh, these mistresses!' she cried. 'To send out a real gentleman like you—with a bandbox—in broad day!'

During this talk they had remained in their original positions—she on the doorstep, he on the sidewalk, bareheaded for the sake of coolness, and with the bandbox on his arm. But upon this last speech, Harry, who was unable to support such point-blank compliments to his appearance, nor the encouraging look with which they were accompanied, began to change his attitude, and glance from left to right in perturbation. In so doing, he turned his face towards the lower end of the lane, and there, to his indescribable dismay, his eyes encountered those of General Vandeleur. The general, in a prodigious fluster of heat, hurry, and indignation, had been scouring the streets in chase of his brother-in-law; but so soon as he caught a glimpse of the delinquent secretary, his purpose changed, his anger flowed into a new channel, and he turned on his heel and came tearing up the lane with truculent gestures and vociferations.

Harry made but one bolt of it into the house, driving the

maid before him; and the door was slammed in his pursuer's countenance.

'Is there a bar? Will it lock?' asked Harry, while a salvo on the knocker made the house echo from wall to wall.

'Why, what is wrong with you?' asked the maid. 'Is it this old gentleman?'

'If he gets hold of me,' whispered Harry, 'I am as good as dead. He has been pursuing me all day, carries a sword-stick, and is an Indian military officer.'

'These are fine manners,' cried the maid. 'And what, if you please, may be his name?'

'It is the general, my master,' answered Harry. 'He is after this bandbox.'

'Did not I tell you?' cried the maid in triumph. 'I told you I thought worse than nothing of your Lady Vandeleur; and if you had an eye in your head you might see what she is for yourself. An ungrateful minx, I will be bound for that!'

The general renewed his attack upon the knocker, and his passion growing with delay, began to kick and beat upon the panels of the door.

'It is lucky,' observed the girl, 'that I am alone in the house; your general may hammer until he is weary, and there is none to open for him. Follow me!'

So saying she led Harry into the kitchen, where she made him sit down, and stood by him herself in an affectionate attitude, with a hand upon his shoulder. The din at the door, so far from abating, continued to increase in volume, and at each blow the unhappy secretary was shaken to the heart.

'What is your name?' asked the girl.

'Harry Hartley,' he replied.

'Mine,' she went on, 'is Prudence. Do you like it?'

'Very much,' said Harry. 'But hear for a moment how the general beats upon the door. He will certainly break it in, and then, in heaven's name, what have I to look for but death?'

'You put yourself very much about with no occasion,' answered Prudence. 'Let your general knock, he will do no more than blister his hands. Do you think I would keep you here if I were not sure to save you? Oh, no, I am a good friend to those that please me! And we have a back door upon another lane. But,' she added, checking him, for he had got upon his feet immediately on this welcome news, 'but I will not show where it is unless you kiss me. Will you, Harry?'

'That I will,' he cried, remembering his gallantry, 'not for your back door, but because you are good and pretty.'

And he administered two or three cordial salutes, which were returned to him in kind.

Then Prudence led him to the back gate, and put her hand upon the key.

'Will you come and see me?' she asked.

'I will indeed,' said Harry. 'Do not I owe you my life?'

'And now,' she added, opening the door, 'run as hard as you can, for I shall let in the general.'

Harry scarcely required this advice; fear had him by the forelock; and he addressed himself diligently to flight. A few steps, and he believed he would escape from his trials, and return to Lady Vandeleur in honour and safety. But these few steps had not been taken before he heard a man's voice hailing him by name with many execrations, and, looking over his shoulder, he beheld Charlie Pendragon waving him with both arms to return. The shock of this new incident was so sudden and profound, and Harry was already worked into so high a state of nervous tension, that he could think of nothing better than to accelerate his pace, and continue running. He should certainly have remembered the scene in Kensington Gardens; he should certainly have concluded that, where the general was his enemy, Charlie Pendragon could be no other than a friend.

But such was the fever and perturbation of his mind that he was struck by none of these considerations, and only continued to run the faster up the lane.

Charlie, by the sound of his voice and the vile terms that he hurled after the secretary, was obviously beside himself with rage. He, too, ran his very best; but, try as he might, the physical advantages were not upon his side, and his outcries and the fall of his lame foot on the macadam began to fall farther and farther into the wake.

Harry's hopes began once more to arise. The lane was both steep and narrow, but it was exceedingly solitary, bordered on either hand by garden walls, overhung with foliage; and, for as far as the fugitive could see in front of him, there was neither a creature moving nor an open door. Providence, weary of persecution, was now offering him an open field for his escape.

Alas! As he came abreast of a garden door under a tuft of chestnuts, it was suddenly drawn back, and he could see inside, upon a garden path, the figure of a butcher's boy with his tray upon his arm. He had hardly recognized the fact before he was some steps beyond upon the other side. But the fellow had had time to observe him; he was evidently much surprised to see a gentleman go by at so unusual a pace; and he came out into the lane and began to call after Harry with shouts of ironical encouragement.

His appearance gave a new idea to Charlie Pendragon, who, although he was now sadly out of breath, once more upraised his voice.

'Stop, thief!' he cried.

And immediately the butcher's boy had taken up the cry and joined in the pursuit.

This was a bitter moment for the hunted secretary. It is true that his terror enabled him once more to improve his pace, and gain with every step on his pursuers; but he was well aware that he was near the end of his resources, and should he meet any one coming the other way, his predicament in the narrow lane would be desperate indeed.

'I must find a place of concealment,' he thought, 'and that within the next few seconds, or all is over with me in this world.'

Scarcely had the thought crossed his mind, than the lane took a sudden turning; and he found himself hidden from his enemies. There are circumstances in which even the least energetic of mankind learn to behave with vigour and decision; and the most cautious forget their prudence and embrace foolhardy resolutions. This was one of those occasions for Harry Hartley; and those who knew him best would have been the most astonished at the lad's audacity. He stopped dead, flung the bandbox over a garden wall, and leaping upward with incredible agility and seizing the copestone with his hands, he tumbled headlong after it into the garden.

He came to himself a moment afterwards, seated in a border of small rosebushes. His hands and knees were cut and bleeding, for the wall had been protected against such an escalade by a liberal provision of old bottles; and he was conscious of a general dislocation and a painful swimming in the head. Facing him across the garden, which was in admirable order, and set with flowers of the most delicious perfume, he beheld the back of a house. It was of considerable extent, and plainly habitable; but, in odd contrast to the grounds, it was crazy, ill-kept, and of a mean appearance. On all other sides the circuit of the garden wall appeared unbroken.

He took in these features of the scene with mechanical glances, but his mind was still unable to piece together or draw a rational conclusion from what he saw. And when he heard footsteps advancing on the gravel, although he turned his eyes in that direction, it was with no thought either for defence or flight.

The newcomer was a large, coarse, and very sordid personage, in gardening clothes, and with a watering-pot in his left hand. One less confused would have been affected with some alarm at the sight of this man's huge proportions and black and lowering eyes. But Harry was too gravely shaken by his fall to be so much as terrified; and if he was unable to divert his glances from the gardener, he remained absolutely passive, and suffered him to draw near, to take him by the shoulder, and to plant him roughly on his feet, without a motion of resistance.

For a moment, the two stared into each other's eyes—Harry fascinated, the man filled with wrath and a cruel, sneering humour.

'Who are you?' he demanded at last. 'Who are you to come flying over my wall and break my Gloire de Dijons! What is your name?' he added, shaking him; 'and what may be your business here?'

Harry could not as much as proffer a word in explanation.

But just at that moment, Pendragon and the butcher's boy went clumping past, and the sound of their feet and their hoarse cries echoed loudly in the narrow lane. The gardener had received his answer; and he looked down into Harry's face with an obnoxious smile.

'A thief!' he said. 'Upon my word, and a very good thing you must make of it; for I see you dressed like a gentleman from top to toe. Are you not ashamed to go about the world in such a trim, with honest folk, I dare say, glad to buy your cast-off finery second hand? Speak up, you dog,' the man went on; 'you can understand English, I suppose; and I mean to have a bit of talk with you before I march you to the station.'

'Indeed, sir,' said Harry, 'this is all a dreadful misconception; and if you will go with me to Sir Thomas Vandeleur's in Eaton Place, I can promise that all will be made plain. The most upright person, as I now perceive, can be led into suspicious positions.'

'My little man,' replied the gardener, 'I will go with you no farther than the station-house in the next street. The inspector, no doubt, will be glad to take a stroll with you as far as Eaton Place, and have a bit of afternoon tea with your great acquaintances. Or would you prefer to go direct to the Home Secretary? Sir Thomas Vandeleur, indeed! Perhaps you think I don't know a gentleman when I see one, from a common run-the-hedge like you? Clothes or no clothes, I can read you like a book. Here is a shirt that maybe cost as much as my Sunday hat; and that coat, I take it, has never seen the inside of Rag-fair, and then your boots—'

The man, whose eyes had fallen upon the ground, stopped short in his insulting commentary, and remained for a moment looking intently upon something at his feet. When he spoke his voice was strangely altered.

'What, in God's name,' said he, 'is all this?'

Harry, following the direction of the man's eyes, beheld a spectacle that struck him dumb with terror and amazement. In his fall he had descended vertically upon the bandbox and burst it open from end to end; thence a great treasure of diamonds had poured forth, and now lay abroad, part trodden in the soil, part scattered on the surface in regal and glittering profusion. There was a magnificent coronet which he had often admired on Lady Vandeleur; there were rings and brooches, ear-drops and bracelets, and even unset brilliants rolling here and there among the rosebushes like drops of morning dew. A princely fortune lay between the two men upon the ground—a fortune in the most inviting, solid, and durable form, capable of being carried in an apron, beautiful in itself, and scattering the sunlight in a million rainbow flashes.

'Good God!' said Harry, 'I am lost!'

His mind raced backwards into the past with the incalculable velocity of thought, and he began to comprehend his day's adventures, to conceive them as a whole, and to recognize the sad imbroglio in which his own character and fortunes had become involved. He looked round him as if for help, but he was alone in the garden, with his scattered diamonds and his redoubtable interlocutor; and when he gave ear, there was no sound but the rustle of the leaves and the hurried pulsation of his heart. It was little wonder if the young man felt himself deserted by his spirits, and with a broken voice repeated his last ejaculation—'I am lost!'

The gardener peered in all directions with an air of guilt; but there was no face at any of the windows, and he seemed to breathe again.

'Pick up a heart,' he said, 'you fool! The worst of it is done. Why could you not say at first there was enough for two? Two?' he repeated, 'aye, and for two hundred! But come away from here, where we may be observed; and, for the love of wisdom, straighten out your hat and brush your clothes. You could not travel two steps the figure of fun you look just now.'

While Harry mechanically adopted these suggestions, the gardener, getting upon his knees, hastily drew together the scattered jewels and returned them to the bandbox. The touch of these costly crystals sent a shiver of emotion through the man's stalwart frame; his face was transfigured, and his eyes shone with concupiscence; indeed it seemed as if he luxuriously prolonged his occupation, and dallied with every diamond that he handled. At last, however, it was done; and, concealing the bandbox in his smock, the gardener beckoned to Harry and preceded him in the direction of the house.

Near the door, they were met by a young man evidently in holy orders, dark and strikingly handsome, with a look of mingled weakness and resolution, and very neatly attired after the manner of his caste. The gardener was plainly annoyed by this encounter; but he put as good a face upon it as he could, and accosted the clergyman with an obsequious and smiling air.

'Here is a fine afternoon, Mr Rolles,' said he: 'a fine afternoon, as sure as God made it! And here is a young friend of mine who had a fancy to look at my roses. I took the liberty to bring him in, for I thought none of the lodgers would object.'

'Speaking for myself,' replied the Reverend Mr Rolles, 'I do not; nor do I fancy any of the rest of us would be more difficult upon so small a matter. The garden is your own, Mr Raeburn; we must none of us forget that; and because you give us liberty to walk there we should be indeed ungracious if we so far presumed upon your politeness as to interfere with the convenience of your friends. But, on second thoughts,' he added, 'I believe that this gentleman and I have met before. Mr Hartley, I think. I regret to observe that you have had a fall.'

And he offered his hand.

A sort of maiden dignity and a desire to delay as long as possible the necessity for explanation moved Harry to refuse this chance of help, and to deny his own identity. He chose the tender mercies of the gardener, who was at least unknown to him, rather than the curiosity and perhaps the doubts of an acquaintance.

'I fear there is some mistake,' said he. 'My name is Thomlinson and I am a friend of Mr Raeburn's.'

'Indeed?' said Mr Rolles. 'The likeness is amazing.'

Mr Raeburn, who had been upon thorns throughout this colloquy, now felt it high time to bring it to a period.

'I wish you a pleasant saunter, sir,' said he.

And with that he dragged Harry after him into the house, and then into a chamber on the garden. His first care was to draw down the blind, for Mr Rolles still remained where they had left him, in an attitude of perplexity and thought.

Then he emptied the broken bandbox on the table, and stood before the treasure, thus fully displayed, with an expression of rapturous greed, and rubbing his hands upon his thighs. For Harry, the sight of the man's face under the influence of this base emotion, added another pang to those he was already suffering. It seemed incredible that, from his life of pure and delicate trifling, he should be plunged in a breath among sordid and criminal relations. He could reproach his conscience with no sinful act; and yet he was now suffering the punishment of sin in its most acute and cruel forms—the dread of punishment, the suspicions of the good, and the companionship and contamination of vile and brutal natures. He felt he could lay his life down with gladness to escape from the room and the society of Mr Raeburn.

'And now,' said the latter, after he had separated the jewels into two nearly equal parts, and drawn one of them nearer to himself; 'and now,' said he, 'everything in this world has to be paid for, and some things sweetly. You must know, Mr Hartley, if such be your name, that I am a man of a very easy temper, and good nature has been my stumbling block from first to last. I could pocket the whole of these pretty pebbles, if I chose, and I should like to see you dare to say a word; but I think I must have taken a liking to you; for I declare I have not the heart to shave you so close. So, do you see, in pure kind feeling, I propose that we divide; and these,' indicating the two heaps, 'are the proportions that seem to me just and friendly. Do you see any objection, Mr Hartley, may I ask? I am not the man to stick upon a brooch.'

'But, sir,' cried Harry, 'what you propose to me is impossible. The jewels are not mine, and I cannot share what is another's, no matter with whom, nor in what proportions.'

'They are not yours, are they not?' returned Raeburn. 'And you could not share them with anybody, couldn't you? Well now, that is what I call a pity; for here am I obliged to take you to the station. The police—think of that,' he continued; 'think of the disgrace for your respectable parents; think,' he went on, taking Harry by the wrist; 'think of the Colonies and the Day of Judgment.'

'I cannot help it,' wailed Harry. 'It is not my fault. You will not come with me to Eaton Place?'

'No,' replied the man, 'I will not, that is certain. And I mean to divide these playthings with you here.'

And so saying, he applied a sudden and severe torsion to the lad's wrist.

Harry could not suppress a scream, and the perspiration burst forth upon his face. Perhaps pain and terror quickened his intelligence, but certainly at that moment the whole business flashed across him in another light; and he saw that there was nothing for it but to accede to the ruffian's proposal, and trust to find the house and force him to disgorge, under more favourable circumstances, and when he himself was clear from all suspicion.

'I agree,' he said.

'There is a lamb,' sneered the gardener. 'I thought you would recognize your interests at last. This bandbox,' he continued, 'I shall burn with my rubbish; it is a thing that curious folk might recognize; and as for you, scrape up your gaieties and put them in your pocket.'

Harry proceeded to obey, Raeburn watching him, and every now and again his greed rekindled by some bright scintillation, abstracting another jewel from the secretary's share, and adding it to his own.

When this was finished, both proceeded to the front door, which Raeburn cautiously opened to observe the street. This was apparently clear of passengers; for he suddenly seized Harry by the nape of the neck, and holding his face downward so that he could see nothing but the roadway and the doorsteps of the houses, pushed him violently before him down one street and up another for the space of perhaps a minute and a half. Harry had counted three corners before the bully relaxed his grasp, and crying, 'Now be off with you!' sent the lad flying head foremost with a well-directed and athletic kick.

When Harry gathered himself up, half stunned and bleeding freely at the nose, Mr Raeburn had entirely disappeared. For the first time, anger and pain so completely overcame the lad's spirits, that he burst into a fit of tears and remained sobbing in the middle of the road.

After he had thus somewhat assuaged his emotion, he began to look about him and read the names of the streets at whose intersection he had been deserted by the gardener. He was still in an unfrequented portion of west London, among villas and large gardens; but he could see some persons at a window who had evidently witnessed his misfortune; and almost immediately after, a servant came running from the house and offered him a glass of water. At the same time, a dirty rogue, who had been slouching somewhere in the neighbourhood, drew near him from the other side.

'Poor fellow,' said the maid, 'how vilely you have been handled, to be sure! Why, your knees are all cut, and your clothes ruined! Do you know the wretch who used you so?'

'That I do!' cried Harry, who was somewhat refreshed by the water; 'and shall run him home in spite of his precautions. He shall pay dearly for this day's work, I promise you.'

'You had better come into the house and have yourself washed and brushed,' continued the maid. 'My mistress will make you welcome, never fear. And see, I will pick up your hat. Why, love of mercy!' she screamed, 'if you have not dropped diamonds all over the street!'

Such was the case; a good half of what remained to him

after the depredations of Mr Raeburn, had been shaken out of his pockets by the somersault and once more lay glittering on the ground. He blessed his fortune that the maid had been so quick of eye; 'there is nothing so bad but it might be worse', thought he; and the recovery of these few seemed to him almost as great an affair as the loss of all the rest. But, alas! As he stooped to pick up his treasures, the loiterer made a rapid onslaught, overset both Harry and the maid with a movement of his arms, swept up a double handful of the diamonds, and made off along the street with an amazing swiftness.

Harry, as soon as he could get upon his feet, gave chase to the miscreant with many cries, but the latter was too fleet of foot, and probably too well acquainted with the locality; for turn where the pursuer would he could find no traces of the fugitive.

In the deepest despondency, Harry revisited the scene of his mishap, where the maid, who was still waiting, very honestly returned him his hat and the remainder of the fallen diamonds. Harry thanked her from his heart, and being now in no humour for economy, made his way to the nearest cab-stand and set off for Eaton Place by coach.

The house, on his arrival, seemed in some confusion, as if a catastrophe had happened in the family; and the servants clustered together in the hall, and were unable, or perhaps not altogether anxious, to suppress their merriment at the tatterdemalion figure of the secretary. He passed them with as good an air of dignity as he could assume, and made directly for the boudoir. When he opened the door, an astonishing and even menacing spectacle presented itself to his eyes; for he beheld the general and his wife and, of all people, Charlie Pendragon, closeted together and speaking with earnestness and gravity on some important subject. Harry saw at once that there was little left for him to explain—plenary confession had plainly been made to the general of the intended fraud upon his pocket, and the unfortunate miscarriage of the scheme; and they had all made common cause against a common danger.

'Thank heaven!' cried Lady Vandeleur, 'here he is! The bandbox, Harry—the bandbox!'

But Harry stood before them silent and downcast.

'Speak!' she cried. 'Speak! Where is the bandbox?'

And the men, with threatening gestures, repeated the demand.

Harry drew a handful of jewels from his pocket. He was very white.

'This is all that remains,' said he. 'I declare before heaven it was through no fault of mine; and if you will have patience, although some are lost, I am afraid, for ever, others, I am sure, may be still recovered.'

'Alas!' cried Lady Vandeleur, 'all our diamonds are gone, and I owe ninety thousand pounds for dress!'

'Madam,' said the general, 'you might have paved the gutter with your own trash; you might have made debts to fifty times the sum you mention; you might have robbed me of my mother's coronet and ring; and Nature might have still so far prevailed that I could have forgiven you at last. But, madam, you have taken the Rajah's Diamond—the Eye of Light, as the Orientals poetically termed it—the Pride of Kashgar! You have taken from me the Rajah's Diamond,' he cried, raising his hands, 'and all, madam, all is at an end between us!'

'Believe me, General Vandeleur,' she replied, 'that is one of the most agreeable speeches that ever I heard from your lips; and since we are to be ruined, I could almost welcome the change, if it delivers me from you. You have told me often enough that I married you for your money; let me tell you now that I always bitterly repented the bargain; and if you were still marriageable, and had a diamond bigger than your head,

I should counsel even my maid against a union so uninviting and disastrous. As for you, Mr Hartley,' she continued, turning on the secretary, 'you have sufficiently exhibited your valuable qualities in this house; we are now persuaded that you equally lack manhood, sense, and self-respect; and I can see only one course open for you—to withdraw instanter, and, if possible, return no more. For your wages, you may rank as a creditor in my late husband's bankruptcy.'

Harry had scarcely comprehended this insulting address, before the general was down upon him with another.

'And in the meantime,' said that personage, 'follow me before the nearest Inspector of Police. You may impose upon a simple-minded soldier, sir, but the eye of the law will read your disreputable secret. If I must spend my old age in poverty through your underhand intriguing with my wife, I mean at least that you shall not remain unpunished for your pains; and God, sir, will deny me a very considerable satisfaction if you do not pick oakum from now until your dying day.'

With that, the general dragged Harry from the apartment, and hurried him downstairs and along the street to the police-station of the district.

Here (says my Arabian author) ended this deplorable business of the bandbox. But to the unfortunate secretary, the whole affair was the beginning of a new and manlier life. The police were easily persuaded of his innocence; and, after he had given what help he could in the subsequent investigations, he was even complimented by one of the chiefs of the detective department on the probity and simplicity of his behaviour. Several persons interested themselves in one so unfortunate; and soon after, he inherited a sum of money from a maiden aunt in Worcestershire. With this, he married Prudence, and set sail for Bendigo, or according to another account, for Trincomalee, exceedingly content, and with the best of prospects.

5

STORY OF THE YOUNG MAN IN HOLY ORDERS

The Reverend Mr Simon Rolles had distinguished himself in the Moral Sciences, and was more than usually proficient in the study of Divinity. His essay 'On the Christian Doctrine of the Social Obligations' obtained for him, at the moment of its production, a certain celebrity in the University of Oxford; and it was understood in clerical and learned circles that young Mr Rolles had in contemplation a considerable work—a folio, it was said—on the authority of the Fathers of the Church. These attainments, these ambitious designs, however, were far from helping him to any preferment; and he was still in quest of his first curacy—when a chance ramble in that part of London, the peaceful and rich aspect of the garden, a desire for solitude and study, and the cheapness of the lodging, led him to take up his abode with Mr Raeburn, the nurseryman of Stockdove Lane.

It was his habit every afternoon, after he had worked seven or eight hours on St. Ambrose or St. Chrysostom, to walk for a while in meditation among the roses. And this was usually one of the most productive moments of his day. But even a sincere appetite for thought, and the excitement of grave problems awaiting solution, are not always sufficient to preserve the mind of the philosopher against the petty shocks and contacts of the world. And when Mr Rolles found General Vandeleur's secretary, ragged and bleeding, in the company of his landlord; when he saw both change colour and seek to avoid his questions; and, above all, when the former denied his own identity with the most unmoved assurance, he speedily forgot the saints and fathers in the vulgar interest of curiosity.

'I cannot be mistaken,' thought he. 'That is Mr Hartley beyond a doubt. How comes he in such a pickle? Why does he deny his name? And what can be his business with that black-looking ruffian, my landlord?'

As he was thus reflecting, another peculiar circumstance attracted his attention. The face of Mr Raeburn appeared at a low window next the door; and, as chance directed, his eyes met those of Mr Rolles. The nurseryman seemed disconcerted, and even alarmed; and immediately after, the blind of the apartment was pulled sharply down.

'This may all be very well,' reflected Mr Rolles; 'it may be all excellently well; but I confess freely that I do not think so. Suspicious, underhand, untruthful, fearful of observation—I believe upon my soul,' he thought, 'the pair are plotting some disgraceful action.'

The detective that there is in all of us awoke and became clamant in the bosom of Mr Rolles; and with a brisk, eager step, that bore no resemblance to his usual gait, he proceeded to make the circuit of the garden. When he came to the scene of Harry's escalade, his eye was at once arrested by a broken rosebush and marks of trampling on the mould. He looked up, and saw scratches on the brick, and a rag of trouser floating from a broken bottle. This, then, was the mode of entrance chosen by Mr Raeburn's particular friend! It was thus that General Vandeleur's secretary came to admire a flower garden!

The young clergyman whistled softly to himself as he stooped to examine the ground. He could make out where Harry had landed from his perilous leap; he recognized the flat foot of Mr Raeburn where it had sunk deeply in the soil as he pulled up the secretary by the collar; nay, on a closer inspection, he seemed to distinguish the marks of groping fingers, as though something had been spilt abroad and eagerly collected.

'Upon my word,' he thought, 'the thing grows vastly interesting.'

And just then, he caught sight of something almost entirely buried in the earth. In an instant he had disinterred a dainty morocco case, ornamented and clasped in gilt. It had been trodden heavily underfoot, and thus escaped the hurried search of Mr Raeburn. Mr Rolles opened the case, and drew a long breath of almost horrified astonishment; for there lay before him, in a cradle of green velvet, a diamond of prodigious magnitude and of the finest water. It was of the bigness of a duck's egg; beautifully shaped, and without a flaw; and as the sun shone upon it, it gave forth a lustre like that of electricity, and seemed to burn in his hand with a thousand internal fires.

He knew little of precious stones; but the Rajah's Diamond was a wonder that explained itself; a village child, if he found it, would run screaming for the nearest cottage; and a savage would prostrate himself in adoration before so imposing a fetish. The beauty of the stone flattered the young clergyman's eyes; the thought of its incalculable value overpowered his intellect. He knew that what he held in his hand was worth more than many years' purchase of an archiepiscopal see; that it would build cathedrals more stately than Ely or Cologne; that he who possessed it was set free for ever from the primal curse, and might follow his own inclinations without concern or hurry, without let or hindrance. And as he suddenly turned it, the rays leaped forth again with renewed brilliancy, and seemed to pierce his very heart.

Decisive actions are often taken in a moment and without any conscious deliverance from the rational parts of man. So it was now with Mr Rolles. He glanced hurriedly round; beheld, like Mr Raeburn before him, nothing but the sunlit flower garden, the tall tree-tops, and the house with blinded windows; and in a trice he had shut the case, thrust it into his pocket, and was hastening to his study with the speed of guilt.

The Reverend Simon Rolles had stolen the Rajah's Diamond.

Early in the afternoon the police arrived with Harry Hartley. The nurseryman, who was beside himself with terror, readily discovered his hoard; and the jewels were identified and inventoried in the presence of the secretary. As for Mr Rolles, he showed himself in a most obliging temper, communicated what he knew with freedom, and professed regret that he could do no more to help the officers in their duty.

'Still,' he added, 'I suppose your business is nearly at an end.'

'By no means,' replied the man from Scotland Yard; and he narrated the second robbery of which Harry had been the immediate victim, and gave the young clergyman a description of the more important jewels that were still not found, dilating particularly on the Rajah's Diamond.

'It must be worth a fortune,' observed Mr Rolles.

'Ten fortunes—twenty fortunes,' cried the officer.

'The more it is worth,' remarked Simon shrewdly, 'the more difficult it must be to sell. Such a thing has a physiognomy not to be disguised, and I should fancy a man might as easily negotiate St. Paul's Cathedral.'

'Oh, truly!' said the officer; 'but if the thief be a man of any intelligence, he will cut it into three or four, and there will be still enough to make him rich.'

'Thank you,' said the clergyman. 'You cannot imagine how

much your conversation interests me.'

Whereupon the functionary admitted that they knew many strange things in his profession, and immediately after took his leave.

Mr Rolles regained his apartment. It seemed smaller and barer than usual; the materials for his great work had never presented so little interest; and he looked upon his library with the eye of scorn. He took down, volume by volume, several Fathers of the Church, and glanced them through; but they contained nothing to his purpose.

'These old gentlemen,' thought he, 'are no doubt very valuable writers, but they seem to me conspicuously ignorant of life. Here am I, with learning enough to be a bishop, and I positively do not know how to dispose of a stolen diamond. I glean a hint from a common policeman, and, with all my folios, I cannot so much as put it into execution. This inspires me with very low ideas of University training.'

Herewith he kicked over his bookshelf and, putting on his hat, hastened from the house to the club of which he was a member. In such a place of mundane resort he hoped to find some man of good counsel and a shrewd experience in life. In the reading room he saw many of the country clergy and an Archdeacon; there were three journalists and a writer upon the Higher Metaphysic, playing pool; and at dinner only the raff of ordinary club frequenters showed their commonplace and obliterated countenances. None of these, thought Mr Rolles, would know more on dangerous topics than he knew himself; none of them were fit to give him guidance in his present strait. At length in the smoking room, up many weary stairs, he hit upon a gentleman of somewhat portly build and dressed with conspicuous plainness. He was smoking a cigar and reading the *Fortnightly Review*; his face was singularly free from all sign of preoccupation or fatigue; and there was something in his air which seemed to invite confidence and to expect submission. The more the young clergyman scrutinized his features, the more he was convinced that he had fallen on one capable of giving pertinent advice.

'Sir,' said he, 'you will excuse my abruptness; but I judge you from your appearance to be pre-eminently a man of the world.'

'I have indeed considerable claims to that distinction,' replied the stranger, laying aside his magazine with a look of mingled amusement and surprise.

'I, sir,' continued the curate, 'am a recluse, a student, a creature of ink bottles and patristic folios. A recent event has brought my folly vividly before my eyes, and I desire to instruct myself in life. By life,' he added, 'I do not mean Thackeray's novels; but the crimes and secret possibilities of our society, and the principles of wise conduct among exceptional events. I am a patient reader; can the thing be learnt in books?'

'You put me in a difficulty,' said the stranger. 'I confess I have no great notion of the use of books, except to amuse a railway journey; although, I believe, there are some very exact treatises on astronomy, the use of the globes, agriculture, and the art of making paper flowers. Upon the less apparent provinces of life I fear you will find nothing truthful. Yet stay,' he added, 'have you read Gaboriau?'

Mr Rolles admitted he had never even heard the name.

'You may gather some notions from Gaboriau,' resumed the stranger. 'He is at least suggestive; and as he is an author much studied by Prince Bismarck, you will, at the worst, lose your time in good society.'

'Sir,' said the curate, 'I am infinitely obliged by your politeness.'

'You have already more than repaid me,' returned the other.

'How?' inquired Simon.

'By the novelty of your request,' replied the gentleman; and with a polite gesture, as though to ask permission, he resumed the study of the *Fortnightly Review*.

On his way home, Mr Rolles purchased a work on precious stones and several of Gaboriau's novels. These last he eagerly skimmed until an advanced hour in the morning; but although they introduced him to many new ideas, he could nowhere discover what to do with a stolen diamond. He was annoyed, moreover, to find the information scattered amongst romantic storytelling, instead of soberly set forth after the manner of a manual; and he concluded that, even if the writer had thought much upon these subjects, he was totally lacking in educational method. For the character and attainments of Lecoq, however, he was unable to contain his admiration.

'He was truly a great creature,' ruminated Mr Rolles. 'He knew the world as I know Paley's Evidences. There was nothing that he could not carry to a termination with his own hand, and against the largest odds. Heavens!' he broke out suddenly, 'is not this the lesson? Must I not learn to cut diamonds for myself?'

It seemed to him as if he had sailed at once out of his perplexities; he remembered that he knew a jeweller, one B. Macculloch, in Edinburgh, who would be glad to put him in the way of the necessary training; a few months, perhaps a few years, of sordid toil, and he would be sufficiently expert to divide and sufficiently cunning to dispose with advantage of the Rajah's Diamond. That done, he might return to pursue his researches at leisure, a wealthy and luxurious student, envied and respected by all. Golden visions attended him through his slumber, and he awoke refreshed and light-hearted with the morning sun.

Mr Raeburn's house was on that day to be closed by the police, and this afforded a pretext for his departure. He cheerfully prepared his baggage, transported it to King's Cross, where he left it in the cloakroom, and returned to the club to while away the afternoon and dine.

'If you dine here today, Rolles,' observed an acquaintance, 'you may see two of the most remarkable men in England—Prince Florizel of Bohemia, and old Jack Vandeleur.'

'I have heard of the prince,' replied Mr Rolles; 'and General Vandeleur I have even met in society.'

'General Vandeleur is an ass!' returned the other. 'This is his brother John, the biggest adventurer, the best judge of precious stones, and one of the most acute diplomatists in Europe. Have you never heard of his duel with the Duc de Val d'Orge? Of his exploits and atrocities when he was Dictator of Paraguay? Of his dexterity in recovering Sir Samuel Levi's jewellery? Nor of his services in the Indian Mutiny—services by which the Government profited, but which the Government dared not recognize? You make me wonder what we mean by fame, or even by infamy; for Jack Vandeleur has prodigious claims to both. Run downstairs,' he continued, 'take a table near them, and keep your ears open. You will hear some strange talk, or I am much misled.'

'But how shall I know them?' inquired the clergyman.

'Know them!' cried his friend; 'why, the prince is the finest gentleman in Europe, the only living creature who looks like a king; and as for Jack Vandeleur, if you can imagine Ulysses at seventy years of age, and with a sabre-cut across his face, you have the man before you! Know them, indeed! Why, you could pick either of them out of a Derby day!'

Rolles eagerly hurried to the dining room. It was as his friend had asserted; it was impossible to mistake the pair in question. Old John Vandeleur was of a remarkable force of body, and obviously broken to the most difficult exercises. He had neither the carriage of a swordsman, nor of a sailor, nor yet of one much inured to the saddle; but something made up of all these, and the result and expression of many different habits and dexterities. His features were bold and aquiline; his expression arrogant and predatory; his whole appearance that of a swift, violent, unscrupulous man of action; and his copious white hair and the deep sabre-cut that traversed his nose and temple added a note of savagery to a head already remarkable and menacing in itself.

In his companion, the Prince of Bohemia, Mr Rolles was astonished to recognize the gentleman who had recommended him the study of Gaboriau. Doubtless Prince Florizel, who rarely visited the club, of which, as of most others, he was an honorary member, had been waiting for John Vandeleur when Simon accosted him on the previous evening.

The other diners had modestly retired into the angles of the room, and left the distinguished pair in a certain isolation, but the young clergyman was unrestrained by any sentiment of awe, and, marching boldly up, took his place at the nearest table.

The conversation was, indeed, new to the student's ears. The ex-Dictator of Paraguay stated many extraordinary experiences in different quarters of the world; and the prince supplied a commentary which, to a man of thought, was even more interesting than the events themselves. Two forms of experience were thus brought together and laid before the young clergyman; and he did not know which to admire the most—the desperate actor or the skilled expert in life; the man who spoke boldly of his own deeds and perils, or the man who seemed, like a god, to know all things and to have suffered nothing. The manner of each aptly fitted with his part in the discourse. The dictator indulged in brutalities alike of speech and gesture; his hand opened and shut and fell roughly on the table; and his voice was loud and heavy. The prince, on the other hand, seemed the very type of urbane docility and quiet; the least movement, the least inflection, had with him a weightier significance than all the shouts and pantomime of his companion; and if ever, as must frequently have been the case, he described some experience personal to himself, it was so aptly dissimulated as to pass unnoticed with the rest.

At length, the talk wandered on to the late robberies and the Rajah's Diamond.

'That diamond would be better in the sea,' observed Prince Florizel.

'As a Vandeleur,' replied the dictator, 'your Highness may imagine my dissent.'

'I speak on grounds of public policy,' pursued the prince. 'Jewels so valuable should be reserved for the collection of a prince or the treasury of a great nation. To hand them about among the common sort of men is to set a price on virtue's head; and if the Rajah of Kashgar—a prince, I understand, of great enlightenment—desired vengeance upon the men of Europe, he could hardly have gone more efficaciously about his purpose than by sending us this apple of discord. There is no honesty too robust for such a trial. I myself, who have many duties and many privileges of my own—I myself, Mr Vandeleur, could scarce handle the intoxicating crystal and be safe. As for you, who are a diamond hunter by taste and profession, I do not believe there is a crime in the calendar you would not perpetrate—I do not believe you have a friend in the world whom you would not eagerly betray—I do not know if you have a family, but if you have I declare you would sacrifice your children—and all this for what? Not to be richer, nor to have more comforts or more respect, but simply to call this diamond yours for a year or two until you die, and now and again to open a safe and look at it as one looks at a picture.'

'It is true,' replied Vandeleur. 'I have hunted most things, from men and women down to mosquitos; I have dived for coral; I have followed both whales and tigers; and a diamond is the tallest quarry of the lot. It has beauty and worth; it alone can properly reward the ardours of the chase. At this moment, as your Highness may fancy, I am upon the trail; I have a sure knack, a wide experience; I know every stone of price in my brother's collection as a shepherd knows his sheep; and I wish I may die if I do not recover them every one!'

'Sir Thomas Vandeleur will have great cause to thank you,' said the prince.

'I am not so sure,' returned the dictator, with a laugh. 'One of the Vandeleurs will. Thomas or John—Peter or Paul—we are all apostles.'

'I did not catch your observation,' said the prince with some disgust.

And at the same moment, the waiter informed Mr Vandeleur that his cab was at the door.

Mr Rolles glanced at the clock, and saw that he also must be moving; and the coincidence struck him sharply and unpleasantly, for he desired to see no more of the diamond hunter.

Much study having somewhat shaken the young man's nerves, he was in the habit of travelling in the most luxurious manner; and for the present journey he had taken a sofa in the sleeping carriage.

'You will be very comfortable,' said the guard; 'there is no one in your compartment, and only one old gentleman in the other end.'

It was close upon the hour, and the tickets were being examined, when Mr Rolles beheld this other fellow-passenger ushered by several porters into his place; certainly, there was not another man in the world whom he would not have preferred— for it was old John Vandeleur, the ex-dictator.

The sleeping carriages on the Great Northern line were divided into three compartments—one at each end for travellers, and one in the centre fitted with the conveniences of a lavatory. A door running in grooves separated each of the others from the lavatory; but as there were neither bolts nor locks, the whole suite was practically common ground.

When Mr Rolles had studied his position, he perceived himself without defence. If the dictator chose to pay him a visit in the course of the night, he could do no less than receive it; he had no means of fortification, and lay open to attack as if he had been lying in the fields. This situation caused him some agony of mind. He recalled with alarm the boastful statements of his fellow traveller across the dining table, and the professions of immorality which he had heard him offering to the disgusted prince. Some persons, he remembered to have read, are endowed with a singular quickness of perception for the neighbourhood of precious metals; through walls and even at considerable distances they are said to divine the presence of gold. Might it not be the same with diamonds? he wondered; and if so, who was more likely to enjoy this transcendental sense than the person who gloried in the appellation of the Diamond Hunter? From such a man he recognized that he had everything to fear, and longed eagerly for the arrival of the day.

In the meantime, he neglected no precaution, concealed his diamond in the most internal pocket of a system of greatcoats, and devoutly recommended himself to the care of Providence.

The train pursued its usual even and rapid course; and nearly half the journey had been accomplished before slumber began to triumph over uneasiness in the breast of Mr Rolles. For some time he resisted its influence; but it grew upon him more and more, and a little before York he was fain to stretch himself upon one of the couches and suffer his eyes to close; and almost at the same instant, consciousness deserted the young clergyman. His last thought was of his terrifying neighbour.

When he awoke it was still pitch dark, except for the flicker of the veiled lamp; and the continual roaring and oscillation testified to the unrelaxed velocity of the train. He sat upright in a panic, for he had been tormented by the most uneasy dreams; it was some seconds before he recovered his self-command; and even after he had resumed a recumbent attitude, sleep continued to flee him, and he lay awake with his brain in a state of violent agitation, and his eyes fixed upon the lavatory door. He pulled his clerical felt hat over his brow still farther to shield him from the light; and he adopted the usual expedients, such as counting a thousand or banishing thought, by which experienced invalids are accustomed to woo the approach of sleep. In the case of Mr Rolles they proved one and all vain; he was harassed by a dozen different anxieties—the old man in the other end of the carriage haunted him in the most alarming shapes; and in whatever attitude he chose to lie, the diamond in his pocket occasioned him a sensible physical distress. It burned, it was too large, it bruised his ribs; and there were infinitesimal fractions of a second in which he had half a mind to throw it from the window.

While he was thus lying, a strange incident took place.

The sliding door into the lavatory stirred a little, and then a little more, and was finally drawn back for the space of about twenty inches. The lamp in the lavatory was unshaded, and in the lighted aperture thus disclosed, Mr Rolles could see the head of Mr Vandeleur in an attitude of deep attention. He was conscious that the gaze of the dictator rested intently on his own face; and the instinct of self-preservation moved him to hold his breath, to refrain from the least movement, and keeping his eyes lowered, to watch his visitor from underneath the lashes. After about a moment, the head was withdrawn and the door of the lavatory replaced.

The dictator had not come to attack, but to observe; his action was not that of a man threatening another, but that of a man who was himself threatened; if Mr Rolles was afraid of him, it appeared that he, in his turn, was not quite easy on the score of Mr Rolles. He had come, it would seem, to make sure that his only fellow traveller was asleep; and, when satisfied on that point, he had at once withdrawn.

The clergyman leaped to his feet. The extreme of terror had given place to a reaction of foolhardy daring. He reflected that the rattle of the flying train concealed all other sounds, and determined, come what might, to return the visit he had just received. Divesting himself of his cloak, which might have interfered with the freedom of his action, he entered the lavatory and paused to listen. As he had expected, there was nothing to be heard above the roar of the train's progress; and laying his hand on the door at the farther side, he proceeded cautiously to draw it back for about six inches. Then he stopped, and could not contain an ejaculation of surprise.

John Vandeleur wore a fur travelling cap with lappets to protect his ears; and this may have combined with the sound of the express to keep him in ignorance of what was going forward. It is certain, at least, that he did not raise his head, but continued without interruption to pursue his strange employment. Between his feet stood an open hatbox; in one hand he held the sleeve of his sealskin greatcoat; in the other a formidable knife, with which he had just slit up the lining of the sleeve. Mr Rolles had read of persons carrying money in a belt; and as he had no acquaintance with any but cricket-belts, he had never been able rightly to conceive how this was managed. But here was a stranger thing before his eyes; for John Vandeleur, it appeared, carried diamonds in the lining of his sleeve; and even as the young clergyman gazed, he could see one glittering brilliant drop after another into the hatbox.

He stood riveted to the spot, following this unusual business with his eyes. The diamonds were, for the most part, small, and not easily distinguishable either in shape or fire. Suddenly, the dictator appeared to find a difficulty; he employed both hands and stooped over his task; but it was not until after considerable manoeuvring that he extricated a large tiara of diamonds from the lining, and held it up for some seconds' examination before he placed it with the others in the hatbox. The tiara was a ray of light to Mr Rolles; he immediately recognized it for a part of the treasure stolen from Harry Hartley by the loiterer. There was no room for mistake; it was exactly as the detective had described it; there were the ruby stars, with a great emerald in the centre; there were the interlacing crescents; and there were the pear-shaped pendants, each a single stone, which gave a special value to Lady Vandeleur's tiara.

Mr Rolles was hugely relieved. The dictator was as deeply in the affair as he was; neither could tell tales upon the other. In the first glow of happiness, the clergyman suffered a deep sigh to escape him; and as his bosom had become choked and his throat dry during his previous suspense, the sigh was followed by a cough.

Mr Vandeleur looked up; his face contracted with the blackest and most deadly passion; his eyes opened widely, and his under jaw dropped in an astonishment that was upon the brink of fury. By an instinctive movement, he had covered the hatbox with the coat. For half a minute the two men stared upon each other in silence. It was not a long interval, but it sufficed for Mr Rolles; he was one of those who think swiftly on dangerous occasions; he decided on a course of action of a singularly daring nature; and although he felt he was setting his life upon the hazard, he was the first to break silence.

'I beg your pardon,' said he.

The dictator shivered slightly, and when he spoke his voice was hoarse.

'What do you want here?' he asked.

'I take a particular interest in diamonds,' replied Mr Rolles, with an air of perfect self-possession. 'Two connoisseurs should be acquainted. I have here a trifle of my own which may perhaps serve for an introduction.'

And so saying, he quietly took the case from his pocket, showed the Rajah's Diamond to the dictator for an instant, and replaced it in security.

'It was once your brother's,' he added.

John Vandeleur continued to regard him with a look of almost painful amazement; but he neither spoke nor moved.

'I was pleased to observe,' resumed the young man, 'that we have gems from the same collection.'

The dictator's surprise overpowered him.

'I beg your pardon,' he said; 'I begin to perceive that I am growing old! I am positively not prepared for little incidents like this. But set my mind at rest upon one point: do my eyes deceive me, or are you indeed a parson?'

'I am in holy orders,' answered Mr Rolles.

'Well,' cried the other, 'as long as I live I will never hear another word against the cloth!'

'You flatter me,' said Mr Rolles.

'Pardon me,' replied Vandeleur; 'pardon me, young man. You are no coward, but it still remains to be seen whether you are not the worst of fools. Perhaps,' he continued, leaning back upon his seat, 'perhaps you would oblige me with a few particulars. I must suppose you had some object in the stupefying impudence of your proceedings, and I confess I have a curiosity to know it.'

'It is very simple,' replied the clergyman; 'it proceeds from my great inexperience of life.'

'I shall be glad to be persuaded,' answered Vandeleur.

Whereupon, Mr Rolles told him the whole story of his connection with the Rajah's Diamond, from the time he found it in Raeburn's garden to the time when he left London in the Flying Scotchman. He added a brief sketch of his feelings and thoughts during the journey, and concluded in these words:-

'When I recognized the tiara I knew we were in the same attitude towards society, and this inspired me with a hope, which I trust you will say was not ill-founded, that you might become in some sense my partner in the difficulties and, of course, the profits of my situation. To one of your special knowledge and obviously great experience, the negotiation of the diamond would give but little trouble, while to me it was a matter of impossibility. On the other part, I judged that I might lose nearly as much by cutting the diamond, and that not improbably with an unskilful hand, as might enable me to pay you with proper generosity for your assistance. The subject was a delicate one to broach; and perhaps I fell short in delicacy. But I must ask you to remember that for me the situation was a new one, and I was entirely unacquainted with the etiquette in use. I believe without vanity that I could have married or baptized you in a very acceptable manner; but every man has his own aptitudes, and this sort of bargain was not among the list of my accomplishments.'

'I do not wish to flatter you,' replied Vandeleur; 'but upon my word, you have an unusual disposition for a life of crime. You have more accomplishments than you imagine; and though I have encountered a number of rogues in different quarters of the world, I never met with one so unblushing as yourself. Cheer up, Mr Rolles, you are in the right profession at last! As for helping you, you may command me as you will. I have only a day's business in Edinburgh on a little matter for my brother; and once that is concluded, I return to Paris, where I usually reside. If you please, you may accompany me thither. And before the end of a month I believe I shall have brought your little business to a satisfactory conclusion.'

At this point, contrary to all the canons of his art, our Arabian author breaks off the STORY OF THE YOUNG MAN IN HOLY ORDERS. I regret and condemn such practices; but I must follow my original, and refer the reader for the conclusion of Mr Rolles' adventures to the next number of the cycle, the STORY OF THE HOUSE WITH THE GREEN BLINDS.

6

STORY OF THE HOUSE WITH THE GREEN BLINDS

Francis Scrymgeour, a clerk in the Bank of Scotland at Edinburgh, had attained the age of twenty-five in a sphere of quiet, creditable, and domestic life. His mother died while he was young; but his father, a man of sense and probity, had given him an excellent education at school, and brought him up at home to orderly and frugal habits. Francis, who was of a docile and affectionate disposition, profited by these advantages with zeal, and devoted himself heart and soul to his employment. A walk upon Saturday afternoon, an occasional dinner with members of his family, and a yearly tour of a fortnight in the Highlands or even on the continent of Europe, were his principal distractions, and, he grew rapidly in favour with his superiors, and enjoyed already a salary of nearly two hundred pounds a year, with the prospect of an ultimate advance to almost double that amount. Few young men were more contented, few more willing and laborious than Francis Scrymgeour. Sometimes at night, when he had read the daily paper, he would play upon the flute to amuse his father, for whose qualities he entertained a great respect.

One day he received a note from a well-known firm of

Writers to the Signet, requesting the favour of an immediate interview with him. The letter was marked 'Private and Confidential', and had been addressed to him at the bank, instead of at home—two unusual circumstances which made him obey the summons with the more alacrity. The senior member of the firm, a man of much austerity of manner, made him gravely welcome, requested him to take a seat, and proceeded to explain the matter in hand in the picked expressions of a veteran man of business. A person, who must remain nameless, but of whom the lawyer had every reason to think well—a man, in short, of some station in the country—desired to make Francis an annual allowance of five hundred pounds. The capital was to be placed under the control of the lawyer's firm and two trustees who must also remain anonymous. There were conditions annexed to this liberality, but he was of opinion that his new client would find nothing either excessive or dishonourable in the terms; and he repeated these two words with emphasis, as though he desired to commit himself to nothing more.

Francis asked their nature.

'The conditions,' said the Writer to the Signet, 'are, as I have twice remarked, neither dishonourable nor excessive. At the same time I cannot conceal from you that they are most unusual. Indeed, the whole case is very much out of our way; and I should certainly have refused it had it not been for the reputation of the gentleman who entrusted it to my care, and, let me add, Mr Scrymgeour, the interest I have been led to take in yourself by many complimentary and, I have no doubt, well-deserved reports.'

Francis entreated him to be more specific.

'You cannot picture my uneasiness as to these conditions,' he said.

'They are two,' replied the lawyer, 'only two; and the sum, as you will remember, is five hundred a year—and unburdened,

I forgot to add, unburdened.'

And the lawyer raised his eyebrows at him with solemn gusto.

'The first,' he resumed, 'is of remarkable simplicity. You must be in Paris by the afternoon of Sunday, the fifteenth; there you will find, at the box-office of the Comedie Francaise, a ticket for admission taken in your name and waiting you. You are requested to sit out the whole performance in the seat provided, and that is all.'

'I should certainly have preferred a weekday,' replied Francis. ' But, after all, once in a way—'

'And in Paris, my dear sir,' added the lawyer soothingly. 'I believe I am something of a precisian myself, but upon such a consideration, and in Paris, I should not hesitate an instant.'

And the pair laughed pleasantly together.

'The other is of more importance,' continued the Writer to the Signet. 'It regards your marriage. My client, taking a deep interest in your welfare, desires to advise you absolutely in the choice of a wife. Absolutely, you understand,' he repeated.

'Let us be more explicit, if you please,' returned Francis. 'Am I to marry any one, maid or widow, black or white, whom this invisible person chooses to propose?'

'I was to assure you that suitability of age and position should be a principle with your benefactor,' replied the lawyer. 'As to race, I confess the difficulty had not occurred to me, and I failed to inquire; but if you like I will make a note of it at once, and advise you on the earliest opportunity.'

'Sir,' said Francis, 'it remains to be seen whether this whole affair is not a most unworthy fraud. The circumstances are inexplicable—I had almost said incredible; and until I see a little more daylight, and some plausible motive, I confess I should be very sorry to put a hand to the transaction. I appeal to you in this difficulty for information. I must learn what is at the bottom of it all. If you do not know, cannot guess, or are not at liberty to tell me, I shall take my hat and go back to my bank as came.'

'I do not know,' answered the lawyer, 'but I have an excellent guess. Your father, and no one else, is at the root of this apparently unnatural business.'

'My father!' cried Francis, in extreme disdain. 'Worthy man, I know every thought of his mind, every penny of his fortune!'

'You misinterpret my words,' said the lawyer. 'I do not refer to Mr Scrymgeour, senior; for he is not your father. When he and his wife came to Edinburgh, you were already nearly one year old, and you had not yet been three months in their care. The secret has been well kept; but such is the fact. Your father is unknown, and I say again that I believe him to be the original of the offers I am charged at present to transmit to you.'

It would be impossible to exaggerate the astonishment of Francis Scrymgeour at this unexpected information. He pled this confusion to the lawyer.

'Sir,' said he, 'after a piece of news so startling, you must grant me some hours for thought. You shall know this evening what conclusion I have reached.'

The lawyer commended his prudence; and Francis, excusing himself upon some pretext at the bank, took a long walk into the country, and fully considered the different steps and aspects of the case. A pleasant sense of his own importance rendered him the more deliberate: but the issue was from the first not doubtful. His whole carnal man leaned irresistibly towards the five hundred a year, and the strange conditions with which it was burdened; he discovered in his heart an invincible repugnance to the name of Scrymgeour, which he had never hitherto disliked; he began to despise the narrow and unromantic interests of his former life; and when once his mind was fairly made up, he walked with a new feeling of strength and freedom, and nourished himself with the gayest anticipations.

He said but a word to the lawyer, and immediately received a cheque for two quarters' arrears; for the allowance was antedated from the first of January. With this in his pocket, he walked home. The flat in Scotland Street looked mean in his eyes; his nostrils, for the first time, rebelled against the odour of broth; and he observed little defects of manner in his adoptive father which filled him with surprise and almost with disgust. The next day, he determined, should see him on his way to Paris.

In that city, where he arrived long before the appointed date, he put up at a modest hotel frequented by English and Italians, and devoted himself to improvement in the French tongue; for this purpose he had a master twice a week, entered into conversation with loiterers in the Champs Elysees, and nightly frequented the theatre. He had his whole toilette fashionably renewed; and was shaved and had his hair dressed every morning by a barber in a neighbouring street. This gave him something of a foreign air, and seemed to wipe off the reproach of his past years.

At length, on the Saturday afternoon, he betook himself to the box-office of the theatre in the Rue Richelieu. No sooner had he mentioned his name than the clerk produced the order in an envelope of which the address was scarcely dry.

'It has been taken this moment,' said the clerk.

'Indeed!' said Francis. 'May I ask what the gentleman was like?'

'Your friend is easy to describe,' replied the official. 'He is old and strong and beautiful, with white hair and a sabre-cut across his face. You cannot fail to recognize so marked a person.'

'No, indeed,' returned Francis; 'and I thank you for your politeness.'

'He cannot yet be far distant,' added the clerk. 'If you make haste you might still overtake him.'

Francis did not wait to be twice told; he ran precipitately from the theatre into the middle of the street and looked in all directions. More than one white-haired man was within sight; but though he overtook each of them in succession, all wanted the sabre-cut. For nearly half an hour he tried one street after another in the neighbourhood, until at length, recognizing the folly of continued search, he started on a walk to compose his agitated feelings; for this proximity of an encounter with him to whom he could not doubt he owed the day had profoundly moved the young man.

It chanced that his way lay up the Rue Drouot and thence up the Rue des Martyrs; and chance, in this case, served him better than all the forethought in the world. For on the outer boulevard he saw two men in earnest colloquy upon a seat. One was dark, young, and handsome, secularly dressed, but with an indelible clerical stamp; the other answered in every particular to the description given him by the clerk. Francis felt his heart beat high in his bosom; he knew he was now about to hear the voice of his father; and making a wide circuit, he noiselessly took his place behind the couple in question, who were too much interested in their talk to observe much else. As Francis had expected, the conversation was conducted in the English language

'Your suspicions begin to annoy me, Rolles,' said the older man. 'I tell you I am doing my utmost; a man cannot lay his hand on millions in a moment. Have I not taken you up, a mere stranger, out of pure goodwill? Are you not living largely on my bounty?'

'On your advances, Mr Vandeleur,' corrected the other.

'Advances, if you choose; and interest instead of goodwill, if you prefer it,' returned Vandeleur angrily. 'I am not here to pick expressions. Business is business; and your business, let me remind you, is too muddy for such airs. Trust me, or leave me alone and find some one else; but let us have an end, for God's sake, of your jeremiads.'

'I am beginning to learn the world,' replied the other, 'and I see that you have every reason to play me false, and not one to deal honestly. I am not here to pick expressions either; you wish the diamond for yourself; you know you do—you dare not deny it. Have you not already forged my name, and searched my lodging in my absence? I understand the cause of your delays; you are lying in wait; you are the diamond hunter, forsooth; and sooner or later, by fair means or foul, you'll lay your hands upon it. I tell you, it must stop; push me much further and I promise you a surprise.'

'It does not become you to use threats,' returned Vandeleur. 'Two can play at that. My brother is here in Paris; the police are on the alert; and if you persist in wearying me with your caterwauling, I will arrange a little astonishment for you, Mr Rolles. But mine shall be once and for all. Do you understand, or would you prefer me to tell it you in Hebrew? There is an end to all things, and you have come to the end of my patience. Tuesday, at seven; not a day, not an hour sooner, not the least part of a second, if it were to save your life. And if you do not choose to wait, you may go to the bottomless pit for me, and welcome.'

And so saying, the dictator arose from the bench, and marched off in the direction of Montmartre, shaking his head and swinging his cane with a most furious air; while his companion remained where he was, in an attitude of great dejection.

Francis was at the pitch of surprise and horror; his sentiments had been shocked to the last degree; the hopeful tenderness with which he had taken his place upon the bench was transformed into repulsion and despair; old Mr Scrymgeour, he reflected, was a far more kindly and creditable parent than this dangerous and violent intriguer; but he retained his presence of mind, and suffered not a moment to elapse before he was on the trail of the dictator.

That gentleman's fury carried him forward at a brisk pace, and he was so completely occupied in his angry thoughts, that he never so much as cast a look behind him till he reached his own door.

His house stood high up in the Rue Lepic, commanding a view of all Paris and enjoying the pure air of the heights. It was two storeys high, with green blinds and shutters; and all the windows looking on the street were hermetically closed. Tops of trees showed over the high garden wall, and the wall was protected by Chevaux-De-Frise. The dictator paused a moment while he searched his pocket for a key; and then, opening a gate, disappeared within the enclosure.

Francis looked about him; the neighbourhood was very lonely, the house isolated in its garden. It seemed as if his observation must here come to an abrupt end. A second glance, however, showed him a tall house next door presenting a gable to the garden, and in this gable a single window. He passed to the front and saw a ticket offering unfurnished lodgings by the month; and, on inquiry, the room which commanded the dictator's garden proved to be one of those to let. Francis did not hesitate a moment; he took the room, paid an advance upon the rent, and returned to his hotel to seek his baggage.

The old man with the sabre-cut might or might not be his father; he might or he might not be upon the true scent; but he was certainly on the edge of an exciting mystery, and he promised himself that he would not relax his observation until he had got to the bottom of the secret.

From the window of his new apartment, Francis

Scrymgeour commanded a complete view into the garden of the house with the green blinds. Immediately below him a very comely chestnut with wide boughs sheltered a pair of rustic tables where people might dine in the height of summer. On all sides save one, a dense vegetation concealed the soil; but there, between the tables and the house, he saw a patch of gravel walk leading from the verandah to the garden gate. Studying the place from between the boards of the Venetian shutters, which he durst not open for fear of attracting attention, Francis observed but little to indicate the manners of the inhabitants, and that little argued no more than a close reserve and a taste for solitude. The garden was conventual, the house had the air of a prison. The green blinds were all drawn down upon the outside; the door into the veranda was closed; the garden, as far as he could see it, was left entirely to itself in the evening sunshine. A modest curl of smoke from a single chimney alone testified to the presence of living people.

In order that he might not be entirely idle, and to give a certain colour to his way of life, Francis had purchased *Euclid's Geometry* in French, which he set himself to copy and translate on the top of his portmanteau and seated on the floor against the wall; for he was equally without chair or table. From time to time, he would rise and cast a glance into the enclosure of the house with the green blinds; but the windows remained obstinately closed and the garden empty.

Only late in the evening did anything occur to reward his continued attention. Between nine and ten the sharp tinkle of a bell aroused him from a fit of dozing; and he sprang to his observatory in time to hear an important noise of locks being opened and bars removed, and to see Mr Vandeleur, carrying a lantern and clothed in a flowing robe of black velvet with a skull-cap to match, issue from under the veranda and proceed leisurely towards the garden gate. The sound of bolts and bars was then repeated; and a moment after, Francis perceived the dictator escorting into the house, in the mobile light of the lantern, an individual of the lowest and most despicable appearance.

Half an hour afterwards, the visitor was reconducted to the street; and Mr Vandeleur, setting his light upon one of the rustic tables, finished a cigar with great deliberation under the foliage of the chestnut. Francis, peering through a clear space among the leaves, was able to follow his gestures as he threw away the ash or enjoyed a copious inhalation; and beheld a cloud upon the old man's brow and a forcible action of the lips, which testified to some deep and probably painful train of thought. The cigar was already almost at an end, when the voice of a young girl was heard suddenly crying the hour from the interior of the house.

'In a moment,' replied John Vandeleur.

And, with that, he threw away the stump and, taking up the lantern, sailed away under the veranda for the night. As soon as the door was closed, absolute darkness fell upon the house; Francis might try his eyesight as much as he pleased, he could not detect so much as a single chink of light below a blind; and he concluded, with great good sense, that the bedchambers were all upon the other side.

Early the next morning (for he was early awake after an uncomfortable night upon the floor), he saw cause to adopt a different explanation. The blinds rose, one after another, by means of a spring in the interior, and disclosed steel shutters such as we see on the front of shops; these in their turn were rolled up by a similar contrivance; and for the space of about an hour, the chambers were left open to the morning air. At the end of that time, Mr Vandeleur, with his own hand, once more closed the shutters and replaced the blinds from within.

While Francis was still marvelling at these precautions, the door opened and a young girl came forth to look about her in the garden. It was not two minutes before she re-entered the house, but even in that short time he saw enough to convince him that she possessed the most unusual attractions. His curiosity was not only highly excited by this incident, but his spirits were improved to a still more notable degree. The alarming manners and more than equivocal life of his father ceased from that moment to prey upon his mind; from that moment he embraced his new family with ardour; and whether the young lady should prove his sister or his wife, he felt convinced she was an angel in disguise. So much was this the case that he was seized with a sudden horror when he reflected how little he really knew, and how possible it was that he had followed the wrong person when he followed Mr Vandeleur.

The porter, whom he consulted, could afford him little information; but, such as it was, it had a mysterious and questionable sound. The person next door was an English gentleman of extraordinary wealth, and proportionately eccentric in his tastes and habits. He possessed great collections, which he kept in the house beside him; and it was to protect these that he had fitted the place with steel shutters, elaborate fastenings, and Chevaux-De-Frise along the garden wall. He lived much alone, in spite of some strange visitors with whom, it seemed, he had business to transact; and there was no one else in the house, except Mademoiselle and an old woman servant

'Is Mademoiselle his daughter?' inquired Francis.

'Certainly,' replied the porter. 'Mademoiselle is the daughter of the house; and strange it is to see how she is made to work. For all his riches, it is she who goes to market; and every day in the week you may see her going by with a basket on her arm.'

'And the collections?' asked the other.

'Sir,' said the man, 'they are immensely valuable. More I cannot tell you. Since M. de Vandeleur's arrival, no one in the quarter has so much as passed the door.'

'Suppose not,' returned Francis, 'you must surely have some notion what these famous galleries contain. Is it pictures, silks, statues, jewels, or what?'

'My faith, sir,' said the fellow with a shrug, 'it might be carrots, and still I could not tell you. How should I know? The house is kept like a garrison, as you perceive.'

And then, as Francis was returning disappointed to his room, the porter called him back.

'I have just remembered, sir,' said he. 'M. de Vandeleur has been in all parts of the world, and I once heard the old woman declare that he had brought many diamonds back with him. If that be the truth, there must be a fine show behind those shutters.'

By an early hour on Sunday, Francis was in his place at the theatre. The seat which had been taken for him was only two or three numbers from the left-hand side, and directly opposite one of the lower boxes. As the seat had been specially chosen there was doubtless something to be learned from its position; and he judged by an instinct that the box upon his right was, in some way or other, to be connected with the drama in which he ignorantly played a part. Indeed, it was so situated that its occupants could safely observe him from beginning to end of the piece, if they were so minded; while, profiting by the depth, they could screen themselves sufficiently well from any counter-examination on his side. He promised himself not to leave it for a moment out of sight; and whilst he scanned the rest of the theatre, or made a show of attending to the business of the stage, he always kept a corner of an eye upon the empty box.

The second act had been some time in progress, and was even drawing towards a close, when the door opened and two persons entered and ensconced themselves in the darkest of the shade. Francis could hardly control his emotion. It was Mr

Vandeleur and his daughter. The blood came and went in his arteries and veins with stunning activity; his ears sang; his head turned. He dared not look, lest he should awake suspicion; his play-bill, which he kept reading from end to end and over and over again, turned from white to red before his eyes; and when he cast a glance upon the stage, it seemed incalculably far away, and he found the voices and gestures of the actors to the last degree impertinent and absurd.

From time to time, he risked a momentary look in the direction which principally interested him; and once at least he felt certain that his eyes encountered those of the young girl. A shock passed over his body, and he saw all the colours of the rainbow. What would he not have given to overhear what passed between the Vandeleurs? What would he not have given for the courage to take up his opera glass and steadily inspect their attitude and expression? There, for aught he knew, his whole life was being decided—and he not able to interfere, not able even to follow the debate, but condemned to sit and suffer where he was, in impotent anxiety.

At last, the act came to an end. The curtain fell, and the people around him began to leave their places, for the interval. It was only natural that he should follow their example; and if he did so, it was not only natural but necessary that he should pass immediately in front of the box in question. Summoning all his courage, but keeping his eyes lowered, Francis drew near the spot. His progress was slow, for the old gentleman before him moved with incredible deliberation, wheezing as he went. What was he to do? Should he address the Vandeleurs by name as he went by? Should he take the flower from his button-hole and throw it into the box? Should he raise his face and direct one long and affectionate look upon the lady who was either his sister or his betrothed? As he found himself thus struggling among so many alternatives, he had a vision of his old equable existence in the bank, and was assailed by a thought of regret for the past.

By this time he had arrived directly opposite the box; and although he was still undetermined what to do or whether to do anything, he turned his head and lifted his eyes. No sooner had he done so than he uttered a cry of disappointment and remained rooted to the spot. The box was empty. During his slow advance, Mr Vandeleur and his daughter had quietly slipped away.

A polite person in his rear reminded him that he was stopping the path; and he moved on again with mechanical footsteps, and suffered the crowd to carry him unresisting out of the theatre. Once in the street, the pressure ceasing, he came to a halt, and the cool night air speedily restored him to the possession of his faculties. He was surprised to find that his head ached violently, and that he remembered not one word of the two acts which he had witnessed. As the excitement wore away, it was succeeded by an overmastering appetite for sleep, and he hailed a cab and drove to his lodging in a state of extreme exhaustion and some disgust of life.

Next morning, he lay in wait for Miss Vandeleur on her road to market, and by eight o'clock beheld her stepping down a lane. She was simply, and even poorly, attired; but in the carriage of her head and body there was something flexible and noble that would have lent distinction to the meanest toilette. Even her basket, so aptly did she carry it, became her like an ornament. It seemed to Francis, as he slipped into a doorway, that the sunshine followed and the shadows fled before her as she walked; and he was conscious, for the first time, of a bird singing in a cage above the lane.

He suffered her to pass the doorway, and then, coming forth once more, addressed her by name from behind.

'Miss Vandeleur,' said he.

She turned and, when she saw who he was, became deadly pale.

'Pardon me,' he continued; 'Heaven knows I had no will to startle you; and, indeed, there should be nothing startling in the presence of one who wishes you so well as I do. And, believe me, I am acting rather from necessity than choice. We have many things in common, and I am sadly in the dark. There is much that I should be doing, and my hands are tied. I do not know even what to feel, nor who are my friends and enemies.'

She found her voice with an effort.

'I do not know who you are,' she said.

'Ah, yes! Miss Vandeleur, you do,' returned Francis; 'better than I do myself. Indeed, it is on that, above all, that I seek light. Tell me what you know,' he pleaded. 'Tell me who I am, who you are, and how our destinies are intermixed. Give me a little help with my life, Miss Vandeleur—only a word or two to guide me, only the name of my father, if you will—and I shall be grateful and content.'

'I will not attempt to deceive you,' she replied. 'I know who you are, but I am not at liberty to say.'

'Tell me, at least, that you have forgiven my presumption, and I shall wait with all the patience I have,' he said. 'If I am not to know, I must do without. It is cruel, but I can bear more upon a push. Only do not add to my troubles the thought that I have made an enemy of you.'

'You did only what was natural,' she said, 'and I have nothing to forgive you. Farewell.'

'Is it to be *farewell*?' he asked.

'Nay, that I do not know myself,' she answered. 'Farewell for the present, if you like.' And with these words she was gone. Francis returned to his lodging in a state of considerable commotion of mind. He made the most trifling progress with his Euclid for that forenoon, and was more often at the window than at his improvised writing table. But beyond seeing the return of Miss Vandeleur, and the meeting between her and her father, who was smoking a Trichinopoli cigar in the veranda, there was nothing notable in the neighbourhood of the house with the green blinds before the time of the midday meal. The young man hastily allayed his appetite in a neighbouring restaurant, and returned with the speed of unallayed curiosity to the house in the Rue Lepic. A mounted servant was leading a saddle-horse to and fro before the garden wall; and the porter of Francis's lodging was smoking a pipe against the doorpost, absorbed in contemplation of the livery and the steeds.

'Look!' he cried to the young man, 'what fine cattle! What an elegant costume! They belong to the brother of M. de Vandeleur, who is now within upon a visit. He is a great man, a general, in your country; and you doubtless know him well by reputation.'

'I confess,' returned Francis, 'that I have never heard of General Vandeleur before. We have many officers of that grade, and my pursuits have been exclusively civil.'

'It is he,' replied the porter, 'who lost the great diamond of the Indies. Of that at least you must have read often in the papers.'

As soon as Francis could disengage himself from the porter, he ran upstairs and hurried to the window. Immediately below the clear space in the chestnut leaves, the two gentlemen were seated in conversation over a cigar. The general, a red, military-looking man, offered some traces of a family resemblance to his brother; he had something of the same features, something, although very little, of the same free and powerful carriage; but he was older, smaller, and more common in air; his likeness was that of a caricature, and he seemed altogether a poor and debile being by the side of the dictator.

They spoke in tones so low, leaning over the table with

every appearance of interest, that Francis could catch no more than a word or two on an occasion. For as little as he heard, he was convinced that the conversation turned upon himself and his own career; several times the name of Scrymgeour reached his ear, for it was easy to distinguish, and still more frequently he fancied he could distinguish the name Francis.

At length the general, as if in a hot anger, broke forth into several violent exclamations.

'Francis Vandeleur!' he cried, accentuating the last word. 'Francis Vandeleur, I tell you.'

The dictator made a movement of his whole body, half affirmative, half contemptuous, but his answer was inaudible to the young man.

Was he the Francis Vandeleur in question? he wondered. Were they discussing the name under which he was to be married? Or was the whole affair a dream and a delusion of his own conceit and self-absorption?

After another interval of inaudible talk, dissension seemed again to arise between the couple underneath the chestnut, and again the general raised his voice angrily so as to be audible to Francis.

'My wife?' he cried. 'I have done with my wife for good. I will not hear her name. I am sick of her very name.'

And he swore aloud and beat the table with his fist.

The dictator appeared, by his gestures, to pacify him after a paternal fashion; and a little after he conducted him to the garden gate. The pair shook hands affectionately enough; but as soon as the door had closed behind his visitor, John Vandeleur fell into a fit of laughter which sounded unkindly and even devilish in the ears of Francis Scrymgeour.

So another day had passed, and little more learnt. But the young man remembered that the morrow was Tuesday, and promised himself some curious discoveries; all might be well, or all might be ill; he was sure, at least, to glean some curious information, and, perhaps, by good luck, get at the heart of the mystery which surrounded his father and his family.

As the hour of the dinner drew near, many preparations were made in the garden of the house with the green blinds. That table, which was partly visible to Francis through the chestnut leaves, was destined to serve as a sideboard, and carried relays of plates and the materials for salad: the other, which was almost entirely concealed, had been set apart for the diners, and Francis could catch glimpses of white cloth and silver plate.

Mr Rolles arrived, punctual to the minute; he looked like a man upon his guard, and spoke low and sparingly. The dictator, on the other hand, appeared to enjoy an unusual flow of spirits; his laugh, which was youthful and pleasant to hear, sounded frequently from the garden; by the modulation and the changes of his voice it was obvious that he told many droll stories and imitated the accents of a variety of different nations; and before he and the young clergyman had finished their vermouth, all feeling of distrust was at an end, and they were talking together like a pair of school companions.

At length, Miss Vandeleur made her appearance, carrying the soup tureen. Mr Rolles ran to offer her assistance which she laughingly refused; and there was an interchange of pleasantries among the trio which seemed to have reference to this primitive manner of waiting by one of the company.

'One is more at one's ease,' Mr Vandeleur was heard to declare.

Next moment, they were all three in their places, and Francis could see as little as he could hear of what passed. But the dinner seemed to go merrily; there was a perpetual babble of voices and sound of knives and forks below the chestnut; and Francis, who had no more than a roll to gnaw, was affected with envy by the comfort and deliberation of the meal. The party lingered over one dish after another, and then over a delicate dessert, with a bottle of old wine carefully uncorked by the hand of the dictator himself. As it began to grow dark, a lamp was set upon the table and a couple of candles on the sideboard; for the night was perfectly pure, starry, and windless. Light overflowed besides from the door and window in the veranda, so that the garden was fairly illuminated and the leaves twinkled in the darkness.

For perhaps the tenth time, Miss Vandeleur entered the house; and on this occasion she returned with the coffee tray, which she placed upon the sideboard. At the same moment her father rose from his seat.

'The coffee is my province,' Francis heard him say.

And the next moment he saw his supposed father standing by the sideboard in the light of the candles.

Talking over his shoulder all the while, Mr Vandeleur poured out two cups of the brown stimulant, and then, by a rapid act of prestidigitation, emptied the contents of a tiny phial into the smaller of the two. The thing was so swiftly done that even Francis, who looked straight into his face, had hardly time to perceive the movement before it was completed. And next instant, and still laughing, Mr Vandeleur had turned again towards the table with a cup in either hand.

'Ere we have done with this,' said he, 'we may expect our famous Hebrew.'

It would be impossible to depict the confusion and distress of Francis Scrymgeour. He saw foul play going forward before his eyes, and he felt bound to interfere, but knew not how. It might be a mere pleasantry, and then how should he look if he were to offer an unnecessary warning? Or again, if it were serious, the criminal might be his own father, and then how should he not lament if he were to bring ruin on the author of his days? For the first time, he became conscious of his own position as a spy. To wait inactive at such a juncture and with such a conflict of sentiments in his bosom, was to suffer the most acute torture; he clung to the bars of the shutters, his heart beat fast and with irregularity, and he felt a strong sweat break forth upon his body.

Several minutes passed.

He seemed to perceive the conversation die away and grow less and less in vivacity and volume; but still no sign of any alarming or even notable event.

Suddenly the ring of a glass breaking was followed by a faint and dull sound, as of a person who should have fallen forward with his head upon the table. At the same moment, a piercing scream rose from the garden.

'What have you done?' cried Miss Vandeleur. 'He is dead!'

The dictator replied in a violent whisper, so strong and sibilant that every word was audible to the watcher at the window.

'Silence!' said Mr Vandeleur; 'the man is as well as I am. Take him by the heels whilst I carry him by the shoulders.'

Francis heard Miss Vandeleur break forth into a passion of tears.

'Do you hear what I say?' resumed the dictator, in the same tones. 'Or do you wish to quarrel with me? I give you your choice, Miss Vandeleur.'

There was another pause, and the dictator spoke again.

'Take that man by the heels,' he said. 'I must have him brought into the house. If I were a little younger, I could help myself against the world. But now that years and dangers are upon me and my hands are weakened, I must turn to you for aid.'

'It is a crime,' replied the girl.

'I am your father,' said Mr Vandeleur.

This appeal seemed to produce its effect. A scuffling noise

followed upon the gravel, a chair was overset, and then Francis saw the father and daughter stagger across the walk and disappear under the veranda, bearing the inanimate body of Mr Rolles embraced about the knees and shoulders. The young clergyman was limp and pallid, and his head rolled upon his shoulders at every step.

Was he alive or dead? Francis, in spite of the dictator's declaration, inclined to the latter view. A great crime had been committed; a great calamity had fallen upon the inhabitants of the house with the green blinds. To his surprise, Francis found all horror for the deed swallowed up in sorrow for a girl and an old man whom he judged to be in the height of peril. A tide of generous feeling swept into his heart; he, too, would help his father against man and mankind, against fate and justice; and casting open the shutters, he closed his eyes and threw himself with outstretched arms into the foliage of the chestnut.

Branch after branch slipped from his grasp or broke under his weight; then he caught a stalwart bough under his armpit, and hung suspended for a second; and then he let himself drop and fell heavily against the table. A cry of alarm from the house warned him that his entrance had not been effected unobserved. He recovered himself with a stagger, and in three bounds crossed the intervening space and stood before the door in the veranda.

In a small apartment, carpeted with matting and surrounded by glazed cabinets full of rare and costly curios, Mr Vandeleur was stooping over the body of Mr Rolles. He raised himself as Francis entered, and there was an instantaneous passage of hands. It was the business of a second; as fast as an eye can wink the thing was done; the young man had not the time to be sure, but it seemed to him as if the dictator had taken something from the curate's breast, looked at it for the least fraction of time as it lay in his hand, and then suddenly and swiftly passed it to his daughter.

All this was over while Francis had still one foot upon the threshold, and the other raised in air. The next instant he was on his knees to Mr Vandeleur.

'Father!' he cried. 'Let me too help you. I will do what you wish and ask no questions; I will obey you with my life; treat me as a son, and you will find I have a son's devotion.'

A deplorable explosion of oaths was the dictator's first reply.

'Son and father?' he cried. 'Father and son? What d—d unnatural comedy is all this? How do you come in my garden? What do you want? And who, in God's name, are you?'

Francis, with a stunned and shamefaced aspect, got upon his feet again, and stood in silence.

Then a light seemed to break upon Mr Vandeleur, and he laughed aloud

'I see,' cried he. 'It is the Scrymgeour. Very well, Mr Scrymgeour. Let me tell you in a few words how you stand. You have entered my private residence by force, or perhaps by fraud, but certainly with no encouragement from me; and you come at a moment of some annoyance, a guest having fainted at my table, to besiege me with your protestations. You are no son of mine. You are my brother's bastard by a fishwife, if you want to know. I regard you with an indifference closely bordering on aversion; and from what I now see of your conduct, I judge your mind to be exactly suitable to your exterior. I recommend you these mortifying reflections for your leisure; and, in the meantime, let me beseech you to rid us of your presence. If I were not occupied,' added the dictator, with a terrifying oath, 'I should give you the unholiest drubbing ere you went!'

Francis listened in profound humiliation. He would have fled had it been possible; but as he had no means of leaving the residence into which he had so unfortunately penetrated, he could do no more than stand foolishly where he was.

It was Miss Vandeleur who broke the silence.

'Father,' she said, 'you speak in anger. Mr Scrymgeour may have been mistaken, but he meant well and kindly.'

'Thank you for speaking,' returned the dictator. 'You remind me of some other observations which I hold it a point of honour to make to Mr Scrymgeour. My brother,' he continued, addressing the young man, 'has been foolish enough to give you an allowance; he was foolish enough and presumptuous enough to propose a match between you and this young lady. You were exhibited to her two nights ago; and I rejoice to tell you that she rejected the idea with disgust. Let me add that I have considerable influence with your father; and it shall not be my fault if you are not beggared of your allowance and sent back to your scrivening ere the week be out.'

The tones of the old man's voice were, if possible, more wounding than his language; Francis felt himself exposed to the most cruel, blighting, and unbearable contempt; his head turned, and he covered his face with his hands, uttering at the same time a tearless sob of agony. But Miss Vandeleur once again interfered in his behalf.

'Mr Scrymgeour,' she said, speaking in clear and even tones, 'you must not be concerned at my father's harsh expressions. I felt no disgust for you; on the contrary, I asked an opportunity to make your better acquaintance. As for what has passed tonight, believe me it has filled my mind with both pity and esteem.'

Just then Mr Rolles made a convulsive movement with his arm, which convinced Francis that he was only drugged, and was beginning to throw off the influence of the opiate. Mr Vandeleur stooped over him and examined his face for an instant.

'Come, come!' cried he, raising his head. 'Let there be an end of this. And since you are so pleased with his conduct, Miss

Vandeleur, take a candle and show the bastard out.'

The young lady hastened to obey.

'Thank you,' said Francis, as soon as he was alone with her in the garden. 'I thank you from my soul. This has been the bitterest evening of my life, but it will have always one pleasant recollection.'

'I spoke as I felt,' she replied, 'and in justice to you. It made my heart sorry that you should be so unkindly used.'

By this time they had reached the garden gate; and Miss Vandeleur, having set the candle on the ground, was already unfastening the bolts.

'One word more,' said Francis. 'This is not for the last time—I shall see you again, shall I not?'

'Alas!' she answered. 'You have heard my father. What can I do but obey?'

'Tell me at least that it is not with your consent,' returned Francis; 'tell me that you have no wish to see the last of me.'

'Indeed,' replied she, 'I have none. You seem to me both brave and honest.'

'Then,' said Francis, 'give me a keepsake.'

She paused for a moment, with her hand upon the key; for the various bars and bolts were all undone, and there was nothing left but to open the lock.

'If I agree,' she said, 'will you promise to do as I tell you from point to point?'

'Can you ask?' replied Francis. 'I would do so willingly on your bare word.'

She turned the key and threw open the door.

'Be it so,' said she. 'You do not know what you ask, but be it so. Whatever you hear,' she continued, 'whatever happens, do not return to this house; hurry fast until you reach the lighted and populous quarters of the city; even there be upon your guard. You are in a greater danger than you fancy. Promise me you will not so much as look at my keepsake until you are in a place of safety.'

'I promise,' replied Francis.

She put something loosely wrapped in a handkerchief into the young man's hand; and at the same time, with more strength than he could have anticipated, she pushed him into the street.

'Now, run!' she cried.

He heard the door close behind him, and the noise of the bolts being replaced.

'My faith,' said he, 'since I have promised!'

And he took to his heels down the lane that leads into the Rue Ravignan.

He was not fifty paces from the house with the green blinds when the most diabolical outcry suddenly arose out of the stillness of the night. Mechanically he stood still; another passenger followed his example; in the neighbouring floors he saw people crowding to the windows; a conflagration could not have produced more disturbance in this empty quarter. And yet it seemed to be all the work of a single man, roaring between grief and rage, like a lioness robbed of her whelps; and Francis was surprised and alarmed to hear his own name shouted with English imprecations to the wind.

His first movement was to return to the house; his second, as he remembered Miss Vandeleur's advice, to continue his flight with greater expedition than before; and he was in the act of turning to put his thought in action, when the dictator, bareheaded, bawling aloud, his white hair blowing about his head, shot past him like a ball out of the cannon's mouth, and went careering down the street.

'That was a close shave,' thought Francis to himself. 'What he wants with me, and why he should be so disturbed, I cannot think; but he is plainly not good company for the moment, and

I cannot do better than follow Miss Vandeleur's advice.'

So saying, he turned to retrace his steps, thinking to double and descend by the Rue Lepic itself while his pursuer should continue to follow after him on the other line of street. The plan was ill-devised: as a matter of fact, he should have taken his seat in the nearest cafe, and waited there until the first heat of the pursuit was over. But besides that Francis had no experience and little natural aptitude for the small war of private life, he was so unconscious of any evil on his part, that he saw nothing to fear beyond a disagreeable interview. And to disagreeable interviews he felt he had already served his apprenticeship that evening; nor could he suppose that Miss Vandeleur had left anything unsaid. Indeed, the young man was sore both in body and mind—the one was all bruised, the other was full of smarting arrows; and he owned to himself that Mr Vandeleur was master of a very deadly tongue.

The thought of his bruises reminded him that he had not only come without a hat, but that his clothes had considerably suffered in his descent through the chestnut. At the first magazine he purchased a cheap wideawake, and had the disorder of his toilet summarily repaired. The keepsake, still rolled in the handkerchief, he thrust in the meanwhile into his trousers pocket.

Not many steps beyond the shop he was conscious of a sudden shock, a hand upon his throat, an infuriated face close to his own, and an open mouth bawling curses in his ear. The dictator, having found no trace of his quarry, was returning by the other way. Francis was a stalwart young fellow; but he was no match for his adversary whether in strength or skill; and after a few ineffectual struggles he resigned himself entirely to his captor.

'What do you want with me?' said he.

'We will talk of that at home,' returned the dictator grimly.

And he continued to march the young man uphill in the direction of the house with the green blinds.

But Francis, although he no longer struggled, was only waiting an opportunity to make a bold push for freedom. With a sudden jerk he left the collar of his coat in the hands of Mr Vandeleur, and once more made off at his best speed in the direction of the Boulevards.

The tables were now turned. If the dictator was the stronger, Francis, in the top of his youth, was the more fleet of foot, and he had soon effected his escape among the crowds. Relieved for a moment, but with a growing sentiment of alarm and wonder in his mind, be walked briskly until he debauched upon the Place de l'Opera, lit up like day with electric lamps.

'This, at least,' thought he, 'should satisfy Miss Vandeleur.'

And turning to his right along the Boulevards, he entered the Café Américain and ordered some beer. It was both late and early for the majority of the frequenters of the establishment. Only two or three persons, all men, were dotted here and there at separate tables in the hall; and Francis was too much occupied by his own thoughts to observe their presence.

He drew the handkerchief from his pocket. The object wrapped in it proved to be a morocco case, clasped and ornamented in gilt, which opened by means of a spring, and disclosed to the horrified young man a diamond of monstrous bigness and extraordinary brilliancy. The circumstance was so inexplicable, the value of the stone was plainly so enormous, that Francis sat staring into the open casket without movement, without conscious thought, like a man stricken suddenly with idiocy.

A hand was laid upon his shoulder, lightly but firmly, and a quiet voice, which yet had in it the ring of command, uttered these words in his ear—

'Close the casket, and compose your face.'

Looking up, he beheld a man, still young, of an urbane and tranquil presence, and dressed with rich simplicity. This personage had risen from a neighbouring table, and, bringing his glass with him, had taken a seat beside Francis.

'Close the casket,' repeated the stranger, 'and put it quietly back into your pocket, where I feel persuaded it should never have been. Try, if you please, to throw off your bewildered air, and act as though I were one of your acquaintances whom you had met by chance. So! Touch glasses with me. That is better. I fear, sir, you must be an amateur.'

And the stranger pronounced these last words with a smile of peculiar meaning, leaned back in his seat and enjoyed a deep inhalation of tobacco.

'For God's sake,' said Francis, 'tell me who you are and what this means? Why I should obey your most unusual suggestions I am sure I know not; but the truth is, I have fallen this evening into so many perplexing adventures, and all I meet conduct themselves so strangely, that I think I must either have gone mad or wandered into another planet. Your face inspires me with confidence; you seem wise, good, and experienced; tell me, for heaven's sake, why you accost me in so odd a fashion?'

'All in due time,' replied the stranger. 'But I have the first hand, and you must begin by telling me how the Rajah's Diamond is in your possession.'

'The Rajah's Diamond!' echoed Francis.

'I would not speak so loud, if I were you,' returned the other. 'But most certainly you have the Rajah's Diamond in your pocket. I have seen and handled it a score of times in Sir Thomas Vandeleur's collection.'

'Sir Thomas Vandeleur! The General! My father!' cried Francis.

'Your father?' repeated the stranger. 'I was not aware the general had any family.'

'I am illegitimate, sir,' replied Francis, with a flush.

The other bowed with gravity. It was a respectful bow, as of a man silently apologizing to his equal; and Francis felt relieved and comforted, he scarce knew why. The society of this person did him good; he seemed to touch firm ground; a strong feeling of respect grew up in his bosom, and mechanically he removed his wideawake as though in the presence of a superior.

'I perceive,' said the stranger, 'that your adventures have not all been peaceful. Your collar is torn, your face is scratched, you have a cut upon your temple; you will, perhaps, pardon my curiosity when I ask you to explain how you came by these injuries, and how you happen to have stolen property to an enormous value in your pocket.'

'I must differ from you!' returned Francis hotly. 'I possess no stolen property. And if you refer to the diamond, it was given to me not an hour ago by Miss Vandeleur in the Rue Lepic.'

'By Miss Vandeleur of the Rue Lepic!' repeated the other. 'You interest me more than you suppose. Pray continue.'

'Heavens!' cried Francis.

His memory had made a sudden bound. He had seen Mr Vandeleur take an article from the breast of his drugged visitor, and that article, he was now persuaded, was a morocco case.

'You have a light?' inquired the stranger.

'Listen,' replied Francis. 'I know not who you are, but I believe you to be worthy of confidence and helpful; I find myself in strange waters; I must have counsel and support, and since you invite me I shall tell you all.'

And he briefly recounted his experiences since the day when he was summoned from the bank by his lawyer.

'Yours is indeed a remarkable history,' said the stranger, after the young man had made an end of his narrative; 'and your position is full of difficulty and peril. Many would counsel you to seek out your father, and give the diamond to him; but I have other views.

Waiter!' he cried.

The waiter drew near.

'Will you ask the manager to speak with me a moment?' said he; and Francis observed once more, both in his tone and manner, the evidence of a habit of command.

The waiter withdrew, and returned in a moment with manager, who bowed with obsequious respect.

'What,' said he, 'can I do to serve you?'

'Have the goodness,' replied the stranger, indicating Francis, 'to tell this gentleman my name.'

'You have the honour, sir,' said the functionary, addressing young Scrymgeour, 'to occupy the same table with His Highness Prince Florizel of Bohemia.'

Francis rose with precipitation, and made a grateful reverence to the prince, who bade him resume his seat.

'I thank you,' said Florizel, once more addressing the functionary; 'I am sorry to have deranged you for so small a matter.'

And he dismissed him with a movement of his hand.

'And now,' added the prince, turning to Francis, 'give me the diamond.'

Without a word the casket was handed over.

'You have done right,' said Florizel, 'your sentiments have properly inspired you, and you will live to be grateful for the misfortunes of tonight. A man, Mr Scrymgeour, may fall into a thousand perplexities, but if his heart be upright and his intelligence unclouded, he will issue from them all without dishonour. Let your mind be at rest; your affairs are in my hand; and with the aid of heaven I am strong enough to bring them to a good end. Follow me, if you please, to my carriage.'

So saying the prince arose and, having left a piece of gold

for the waiter, conducted the young man from the café and along the Boulevard to where an unpretentious brougham and a couple of servants out of livery awaited his arrival.

'This carriage,' said he, 'is at your disposal; collect your baggage as rapidly as you can make it convenient, and my servants will conduct you to a villa in the neighbourhood of Paris where you can wait in some degree of comfort until I have had time to arrange your situation. You will find there a pleasant garden, a library of good authors, a cook, a cellar, and some good cigars, which I recommend to your attention. Jerome,' he added, turning to one of the servants, 'you have heard what I say; I leave Mr Scrymgeour in your charge; you will, I know, be careful of my friend.'

Francis uttered some broken phrases of gratitude.

'It will be time enough to thank me,' said the prince, 'when you are acknowledged by your father and married to Miss Vandeleur.'

And with that the prince turned away and strolled leisurely in the direction of Montmartre. He hailed the first passing cab, gave an address, and a quarter of an hour afterwards, having discharged the driver some distance lower, he was knocking at Mr Vandeleur's garden gate.

It was opened with singular precautions by the dictator in person.

'Who are you?' he demanded.

'You must pardon me this late visit, Mr Vandeleur,' replied the prince.

'Your Highness is always welcome,' returned Mr Vandeleur, stepping back.

The prince profited by the open space, and without waiting for his host, walked right into the house and opened the door of the salon. Two people were seated there; one was Miss Vandeleur, who bore the marks of weeping about her eyes, and was still shaken from time to time by a sob; in the other the prince recognized the young man who had consulted him on literary matters about a month before, in a club smoking room.

'Good evening, Miss Vandeleur,' said Florizel; 'you look fatigued. Mr Rolles, I believe? I hope you have profited by the study of Gaboriau, Mr Rolles.'

But the young clergyman's temper was too much embittered for speech; and he contented himself with bowing stiffly, and continued to gnaw his lip.

'To what good wind,' said Mr Vandeleur, following his guest, 'am I to attribute the honour of your Highness's presence?'

'I am come on business,' returned the prince; 'on business with you; as soon as that is settled I shall request Mr Rolles to accompany me for a walk—Mr Rolles,' he added with severity, 'let me remind you that I have not yet sat down.'

The clergyman sprang to his feet with an apology; whereupon the prince took an armchair beside the table, handed his hat to Mr Vandeleur, his cane to Mr Rolles, and, leaving them standing and thus menially employed upon his service, spoke as follows:

'I have come here, as I said, upon business; but, had I come looking for pleasure, I could not have been more displeased with my reception nor more dissatisfied with my company. You, sir,' addressing Mr Rolles, 'you have treated your superior in station with discourtesy; you, Vandeleur, receive me with a smile, but you know right well that your hands are not yet cleansed from misconduct—I do not desire to be interrupted, sir,' he added imperiously; 'I am here to speak, and not to listen; and I have to ask you to hear me with respect, and to obey punctiliously. At the earliest possible date your daughter shall be married at the Embassy to my friend, Francis Scrymgeour, your brother's acknowledged son. You will oblige me by offering not less than ten thousand pounds dowry. For yourself, I will indicate to you in writing a mission of some importance in Siam which I destine to your care. And now, sir, you will answer me in two words whether or not you agree to these conditions.'

'Your Highness will pardon me,' said Mr Vandeleur, 'and permit me, with all respect, to submit to him two queries?'

'The permission is granted,' replied the prince.

'Your Highness,' resumed the dictator, 'has called Mr Scrymgeour his friend. Believe me, had I known he was thus honoured, I should have treated him with proportional respect.'

'You interrogate adroitly,' said the prince; 'but it will not serve your turn. You have my commands; if I had never seen that gentleman before tonight, it would not render them less absolute.'

'Your Highness interprets my meaning with his usual subtlety,' returned Vandeleur. 'Once more: I have, unfortunately, put the police upon the track of Mr Scrymgeour on a charge of theft; am I to withdraw or to uphold the accusation?'

'You will please yourself,' replied Florizel. 'The question is one between your conscience and the laws of this land. Give me my hat; and you, Mr Rolles, give me my cane and follow me. Miss Vandeleur, I wish you good evening. I judge,' he added to Vandeleur, 'that your silence means unqualified assent.'

'If I can do no better,' replied the old man, 'I shall submit; but I warn you openly it shall not be without a struggle.'

'You are old,' said the prince; 'but years are disgraceful to the wicked. Your age is more unwise than the youth of others. Do not provoke me, or you may find me harder than you dream. This is the first time that I have fallen across your path in anger; take care that it be the last.'

With these words, motioning the clergyman to follow, Florizel left the apartment and directed his steps towards the garden gate; and the dictator, following with a candle, gave them light, and once more undid the elaborate fastenings with which he sought to protect himself from intrusion.

'Your daughter is no longer present,' said the prince, turning on the threshold. 'Let me tell you that I understand your threats; and you have only to lift your hand to bring upon yourself sudden and irremediable ruin.'

The dictator made no reply; but as the prince turned his back upon him in the lamplight he made a gesture full of menace and insane fury; and the next moment, slipping round a corner, he was running at full speed for the nearest cab-stand.

Here (says my Arabian) the thread of events is finally diverted from THE HOUSE WITH THE GREEN BLINDS. One more adventure, he adds, and we have done with THE RAJAH'S DIAMOND. That last link in the chain is known among the inhabitants of Bagdad by the name of THE ADVENTURE OF PRINCE FLORIZEL AND A DETECTIVE.

7

THE ADVENTURE OF PRINCE FLORIZEL AND A DETECTIVE

Prince Florizel walked with Mr Rolles to the door of a small hotel where the latter resided. They spoke much together, and the clergyman was more than once affected to tears by the mingled severity and tenderness of Florizel's reproaches.

'I have made ruin of my life,' he said at last. 'Help me; tell me what I am to do; I have, alas! neither the virtues of a priest nor the dexterity of a rogue.'

'Now that you are humbled,' said the prince, 'I command no longer; the repentant have to do with God and not with princes. But if you will let me advise you, go to Australia as a colonist, seek menial labour in the open air, and try to forget that you have ever been a clergyman, or that you ever set eyes on that accursed stone.'

'Accurst indeed!' replied Mr Rolles. 'Where is it now? What further hurt is it not working for mankind?'

'It will do no more evil,' returned the prince. 'It is here in my pocket. And this,' he added kindly, 'will show that I place some faith in your penitence, young as it is.'

'Suffer me to touch your hand,' pleaded Mr Rolles.

'No,' replied Prince Florizel, 'not yet.'

The tone in which he uttered these last words was eloquent in the ears of the young clergyman; and for some minutes after the prince had turned away, he stood on the threshold following with his eyes the retreating figure and invoking the blessing of heaven upon a man so excellent in counsel.

For several hours the prince walked alone in unfrequented streets. His mind was full of concern; what to do with the diamond, whether to return it to its owner, whom he judged unworthy of this rare possession, or to take some sweeping and courageous measure and put it out of the reach of all mankind at once and for ever, was a problem too grave to be decided in a moment. The manner in which it had come into his hands appeared manifestly providential; and as he took out the jewel and looked at it under the street lamps, its size and surprising brilliancy inclined him more and more to think of it as of an unmixed and dangerous evil for the world.

'God help me!' he thought; 'if I look at it much oftener, I shall begin to grow covetous myself.'

At last, though still uncertain in his mind, he turned his steps towards the small but elegant mansion on the riverside which had belonged for centuries to his royal family. The arms of Bohemia are deeply graved over the door and upon the tall chimneys; passengers have a look into a green court set with the most costly flowers, and a stork, the only one in Paris, perches on the gable all day long and keeps a crowd before the house. Grave servants are seen passing to and fro within; and from time to time the great gate is thrown open and a carriage rolls below the arch. For many reasons, this residence was especially dear to the heart of Prince Florizel; he never drew near to it without enjoying that sentiment of homecoming so rare in the lives of the great; and on the present evening he beheld its tall roof and mildly illuminated windows with unfeigned relief and satisfaction.

As he was approaching the postern door by which he always entered when alone, a man stepped forth from the shadow and presented himself with an obeisance in the prince's path.

'I have the honour of addressing Prince Florizel of Bohemia?' said he.

'Such is my title,' replied the prince. 'What do you want with me?'

'I am,' said the man, 'a detective, and I have to present your Highness with this billet from the Prefect of Police.'

The prince took the letter and glanced it through by the light of the street lamp. It was highly apologetic, but requested him to follow the bearer to the Prefecture without delay.

'In short,' said Florizel, 'I am arrested.'

'Your Highness,' replied the officer, 'nothing, I am certain, could be further from the intention of the prefect. You will observe that he has not granted a warrant. It is mere formality, or call it, if you prefer, an obligation that your Highness lays on the authorities.'

'At the same time,' asked the prince, 'if I were to refuse to follow you?'

'I will not conceal from your Highness that a considerable discretion has been granted me,' replied the detective with a bow.

'Upon my word,' cried Florizel, 'your effrontery astounds me! Yourself, as an agent, I must pardon; but your superiors shall dearly smart for their misconduct. What, have you any idea, is the cause of this impolitic and unconstitutional act? You will observe that I have as yet neither refused nor consented, and much may depend on your prompt and ingenuous answer. Let me remind you, officer, that this is an affair of some gravity.'

'Your Highness,' said the detective humbly, 'General Vandeleur and his brother have had the incredible presumption to accuse you of theft. The famous diamond, they declare, is in your hands. A word from you in denial will most amply satisfy the prefect; nay, I go farther: if your Highness would so far honour a subaltern as to declare his ignorance of the matter even to myself, I should ask permission to retire upon the spot.'

Florizel, up to the last moment, had regarded his adventure in the light of a trifle, only serious upon international considerations. At the name of Vandeleur the horrible truth broke upon him in a moment; he was not only arrested, but he was guilty. This was not only an annoying incident—it was a peril to his honour. What was he to say? What was he to do? The Rajah's Diamond was indeed an accursed stone; and it seemed as if he were to be the last victim to its influence.

One thing was certain. He could not give the required assurance to the detective. He must gain time.

His hesitation had not lasted a second.

'Be it so,' said he, 'let us walk together to the prefecture.'

The man once more bowed, and proceeded to follow Florizel at a respectful distance in the rear.

'Approach,' said the prince. 'I am in a humour to talk, and, if I mistake not, now I look at you again, this is not the first time that we have met.'

'I count it an honour,' replied the officer, 'that your Highness should recollect my face. It is eight years since I had the pleasure of an interview.'

'To remember faces,' returned Florizel, 'is as much a part of my profession as it is of yours. Indeed, rightly looked upon, a prince and a detective serve in the same corps. We are both combatants against crime; only mine is the more lucrative and yours the more dangerous rank, and there is a sense in which both may be made equally honourable to a good man. I had rather, strange as you may think it, be a detective of character and parts than a weak and ignoble sovereign.'

The officer was overwhelmed.

'Your Highness returns good for evil,' said he. 'To an act of presumption he replies by the most amiable condescension.'

'How do you know,' replied Florizel, 'that I am not seeking to corrupt you?'

'Heaven preserve me from the temptation!' cried the detective.

'I applaud your answer,' returned the prince. 'It is that of a wise and honest man. The world is a great place and stocked with wealth and beauty, and there is no limit to the rewards that may be offered. Such an one who would refuse a million of money may sell his honour for an empire or the love of a woman; and I myself, who speak to you, have seen occasions so tempting, provocations so irresistible to the strength of human virtue, that I have been glad to tread in your steps and recommend myself to the grace of God. It is thus, thanks to that modest and becoming habit alone,' he added, 'that you and I can walk this town together with untarnished hearts.'

'I had always heard that you were brave,' replied the officer, 'but I was not aware that you were wise and pious. You speak the truth, and you speak it with an accent that moves me to the heart. This world is indeed a place of trial.'

'We are now,' said Florizel, 'in the middle of the bridge. Lean your elbows on the parapet and look over. As the water rushing below, so the passions and complications of life carry away the honesty of weak men. Let me tell you a story.'

'I receive your Highness's commands,' replied the man.

And, imitating the prince, he leaned against the parapet, and disposed himself to listen. The city was already sunk in slumber; had it not been for the infinity of lights and the outline of buildings on the starry sky, they might have been alone beside some country river.

'An officer,' began Prince Florizel, 'a man of courage and conduct, who had already risen by merit to an eminent rank, and won not only admiration but respect, visited, in an unfortunate hour for his peace of mind, the collections of an Indian prince. Here he beheld a diamond so extraordinary for size and beauty that from that instant he had only one desire in life: honour, reputation, friendship, the love of country, he was ready to sacrifice all for this lump of sparkling crystal. For three years he served this semi-barbarian potentate as Jacob served Laban; he falsified frontiers, he connived at murders, he unjustly condemned and executed a brother officer who had the misfortune to displease the Rajah by some honest freedoms; lastly, at a time of great danger to his native land, he betrayed a body of his fellow soldiers, and suffered them to be defeated and massacred by thousands. In the end, he had amassed a magnificent fortune, and brought home with him the coveted diamond.

'Years passed,' continued the prince, 'and at length the diamond is accidentally lost. It falls into the hands of a simple and laborious youth, a student, a minister of God, just entering on a career of usefulness and even distinction. Upon him also the spell is cast; he deserts everything, his holy calling, his studies, and flees with the gem into a foreign country. The officer has a brother, an astute, daring, unscrupulous man, who learns the clergyman's secret. What does he do? Tell his brother, inform the police? No; upon this man also the Satanic charm has fallen; he must have the stone for himself. At the risk of murder, he drugs the young priest and seizes the prey. And now, by an accident which is not important to my moral, the jewel passes out of his custody into that of another, who, terrified at what he sees, gives it into the keeping of a man in high station and above reproach.

'The officer's name is Thomas Vandeleur,' continued Florizel. 'The stone is called the Rajah's Diamond. And'—suddenly opening his hand—'you behold it here before your eyes.'

The officer started back with a cry.

'We have spoken of corruption,' said the prince. 'To me this nugget of bright crystal is as loathsome as though it were crawling with the worms of death; it is as shocking as though it were compacted out of innocent blood. I see it here in my hand, and I know it is shining with hell-fire. I have told you but a hundredth part of its story; what passed in former ages, to what crimes and treacheries it incited men of yore, the imagination trembles to conceive; for years and years it has faithfully served the powers of hell; enough, I say, of blood, enough of disgrace, enough of broken lives and friendships; all things come to an end, the evil like the good; pestilence as well as beautiful music; and as for this diamond, God forgive me if I do wrong, but its empire ends tonight.'

The prince made a sudden movement with his hand, and the jewel, describing an arc of light, dived with a splash into the flowing river.

'Amen,' said Florizel with gravity. 'I have slain a cockatrice!'

'God pardon me!' cried the detective. 'What have you done? I am a ruined man.'

'I think,' returned the prince with a smile, 'that many well-to-do people in this city might envy you your ruin.'

'Alas! Your Highness!' said the officer, 'and you corrupt me after all?'

'It seems there was no help for it,' replied Florizel. 'And now let us go forward to the prefecture.'

Not long after, the marriage of Francis Scrymgeour and Miss Vandeleur was celebrated in great privacy; and the prince acted on that occasion as groom's man. The two Vandeleurs surprised some rumour of what had happened to the diamond; and their vast diving operations on the River Seine are the wonder and amusement of the idle. It is true that through some miscalculation they have chosen the wrong branch of the river.

As for the prince, that sublime person, having now served his turn, may go, along with the Arabian author, topsy-turvy into space. But it if the reader insists on more specific information, I am happy to say that a recent revolution hurled him from the throne of Bohemia, in consequence of his continued absence and edifying neglect of public business; and that His Higness now keeps a cigar store in Rupert street, much frequented by other foreign refugees. I go there from time to time to smoke and have a chat, and find him as great a creature as in the days of his prosperity; he has an Olympian air behind the counter; and although a sedentary life is beginning to tell upon his waistcoat, he is probably, take him for all in all, the handsomest tobacconist in London.

ABOUT TERRY O'BRIEN

Terry O'Brien is an academic with three decades of experience in teaching language and communication skills in India and abroad. He also headed a college under the auspices of the University of Delhi.

A prolific writer, with several books to his credit, Terry O'Brien is a reputed professional motivational speaker and a quizmaster.